The Perfect Heart

By

Dawn L. Billings

OTHER BOOKS
BY DAWN L. BILLINGS

Greatness and Children: Learn the Rules

Entitled to Fail, Endowed to Succeed:
America's Journey Back to Greatness

Greatness is Never An Accident

Quotes and Poems of Greatness

What Went Wrong With Our Relationship?
It Started Out So Good

Choose to Be Great Workbook

The ABC's of Great Relationships Workbook

Possibilities II: Stories from the Heart that Feed the Mind

52 Ways to Heal a Relationship

The ABC's of Great Networking

Co-author with her son Corbin:

The ABC's of Becoming Great

The ABC's of Great People Skills

The ABC's-3 set CD Rom versions of books

Possibilities: Awakening the Leadership Potential Within

(featuring: The ABC's of Great Leadership)

The Perfect Heart

By

Dawn L. Billings

Copyright © 2004 by Dawn L. Billings

Published by
Executive Books
206 West Allen Street
Mechanicsburg, PA 17055
717-766-9499   800-233-2665
Fax: 717-766-6565
www.ExecutiveBooks.com

Printed in the United States of America

ISBN 0-937539-83-X

For my sons, Anthony and Corbin,
and my daughter by love, Brigitte Bellini Mungo.

For my sister's by birth and by grace
Syotha Jett, Sue Ellis, Kathy Haworth, Chani Phillips,
Carol Redman, Cheryl Walling, Sandra Pound, JuliAnne
Santiago, and Kristine Sexter.

For my longest, dearest and deepest friends
John and Lucy Hasset, Bonnie and Phil Parker, Larry Crain,
Clare McGinness, and Tim and Randi Collins,

and for my mentors whose gifts were magic,
Dr. Foster Cline, Jim Fay, Charlie "Tremendous" Jones,
Og Mandino, and Jim Stovall.

have known people without eyes who had great vision. I have known people who could not hear that listened carefully," the old man explained. "One person's difficulty can be another's opportunity."

*T*able of *C*ontents

one of us are born perfect," the old man replied. "Perfection is an illusion. Most of us are able to hide our imperfections, our fears, our feelings of inadequacy from others. But now and then the most courageous and best of mankind choose to be born vulnerable. This is the greatest kind of courage, and through such people the rest of us learn compassion and understanding."

One

The Offering and the Miracle

Once upon a time in a faraway land, a great king stood in quiet contemplation. His heart was churning with uncertainty. He and his wife had been warned long ago about this day, and now it had finally arrived. For the first time, the king's heart was glad that his beautiful queen had passed in her sleep a year ago, and that she did not have to share the unbearable fear and confusion crowding in on him now. He knelt in his chambers and made a silent and humble request:

I know that you are watching, dear Caritas, my queen. This is the time we have feared for so long. Be with us now, your daughter and I, as we face this trial with love and courage. You left us well-loved, but we are not as good without you. Please be with both of us through this trying time.

Outside the north castle wall, children were laughing and playing under the shade of the large Empress trees. On any other day the sound of the children's laughter would have touched and healed the king's kind heart, but today there were too many questions and the only answer simply did not make sense.

"Choose the one who though he is blind, can see," was all the old man had said.

Choose the one who though he is blind, can see. What does that mean? the king wondered.

The king's attention was drawn to the noise of the large entry gate opening to the castle. The gates were thick and strong, built of the rich, hard wood from the Empress trees. The Empress trees were the tallest in the land with long, deep green leaves the width of a young child's chest. Because the leaves were in the shape of a heart, the kingdom had become known as Cortellus, or heartland. Cortellus was the only land within thousands of miles where the magnificent trees grew. Their seeds had been the gift of an unusual stranger. Empress trees grew rapidly, almost magically. Their wood was beautiful and strong, and when chopped down they would grow back seven times, while other trees would simply die. The king closed his eyes as he remembered the day the special seeds were given to him by the mysterious old man who brought him news of his greatest joy as well as his present nightmare.

The king was startled from his thoughts as trumpets signaled the arrival of the contestants. Peering over his spacious, marble balcony, the king could see the men lined up to enter. They came from near and far. There were over one hundred in the beginning, before the eliminations. Now there were seven. The king knew to ask each of the men the same question, but his heart was torn. His only daughter was turning twenty-one in a month. This would have been a time of lavish preparation and celebration if it were not for these strange, unfortunate circumstances.

Nearly twenty-two years before, a mysterious old man had arrived at the castle and had requested the presence of the king and queen. He was ushered into to the throne room, where he knelt down humbly. The man refused to disclose where he came from, saying only that he had a message of grave importance.

"King and Queen, you will soon have a daughter," the old man stated.

A baby would be a miracle. The king and queen had been married well over thirty years without being able to conceive a child. They had all but lost hope, and now their joy was overwhelming.

"Your child will be a source of both joy and pain," said the old man. He explained that the princess would be born with a frail heart that would make her unlike other children. She would not be able to run and play, and would be confined to watch others. Her illness would restrict her in many ways, and she would be perceived as weak and frail. The king and queen grew somber and silent, their joy blanketed by the unfortunate prediction.

The old man shook his head. "I have not yet shared the worst news of all," he said. He waited patiently for the king and queen to gain their composure, and then continued. "On your daughter's twenty-first birthday she will die, unless she receives a heart of perfection from one who is willing to sacrifice his heart for her sake."

"How can this be? This is surely too much for us to bear!" cried the queen.

"If the burden is too much for you," comforted the old man, "You can choose not to face it, for this child must be greatly wanted in order to be born."

"But what about her frailty? Would it not be better for her to never have been born, than to be born less than perfect?" asked the king.

"None of us are born perfect," the old man replied.

"Perfection is an illusion. Most of us are able to hide our imperfections, our fears, our feelings of inadequacy from others. But now and then the most courageous and best of mankind choose to be born vulnerable. This is the greatest kind of courage, and through such people the rest of us learn compassion and understanding."

"But we cannot allow her to be born, knowing that she will die," said the queen through her tears.

"Are not all of us born knowing that we will die?" asked the old man.

"But her life will be difficult and confined," argued the king.

"I have known people without eyes who had great vision. I have known people who could not hear that listened care-fully," the old man explained. "One person's difficulty can be another's opportunity. And as for confinement, most confinement is self-imposed." The old man's voice was patient and kind, and his words were as careful as hands cradling a baby for the first time.

"What about her twenty-first birthday? How will we find a person willing to give her the heart that she needs in order to survive? And if we do, what then?" asked the king and queen, desperate for answers.

"Then your daughter will be made strong and whole, and she will rule your kingdom as a great queen for a long time," answered the old man.

"But how do we find the right person willing to give our daughter the heart she needs?" asked the king once again.

"You will have a great contest and the contestants will come from far and wide," the old man answered. "You will shuffle numbers in a deck and allow them to be chosen at random. The men who select the numbers one through seven must not only compete to save the princess's heart, but also be willing to sacrifice their own."

"How long do we have to consider this choice?" asked the queen, as she fought for the breath that was trying to escape her.

"One night," answered the old man. "I must leave in the morning, and I must have your answer before I go."

H *umans are very different than animals or plants. An elephant can only grow to be an elephant; a horse can only grow to be a horse: and when you plant an acorn, it can only grow to be an oak. Mankind, however, was given the ultimate gift—the gift of choice. We, and we alone, choose who and what we will grow to be. We are ultimately defined by our actions, the value we give to our words, and the meaning that we bring to the lives of others."*

T<small>WO</small>

Choosing to Love

The king and queen had always loved the dawn. This morning, though, they were filled with angst because they knew that with the sun came a difficult decision. The king took his queen's hand as the first glimmers of light kissed the new day awake.

"What do you choose, my queen?" he asked. "Do we take the path we know, traveled and worn, or do we take the turn that leads to the mountains and the valleys? One way we will only travel to places we know and understand, while the other will take us to places we have never been, places that will cause our hearts to leap with joy and fall in pain."

"My heart leaves me with no choice, my love," the queen responded. She took the king's hand in hers and raised it softly to her cheek. The king couldn't help but notice the silver in her hair and the tiny age spots that were new to her hands. How many years he had looked at those hands? They were the hands that fed him, held him when he was lost, washed his feet when he couldn't bend, and tenderly rubbed the knots from his neck. How different they were now. The skin on her hands was darkening in small places and thinning, but the graceful beauty of those hands once again captured him. As the queen slowly turned her face to kiss the hand of the man she loved, she raised her eyes to meet his and said, "Love is our only choice. I will accept my daughter as she is. I will love her in her strength and in her weakness. I will treasure the sound of her laughter, and I will hold her as she cries. That is my choice, my dear, but what is yours?"

"My choice is to walk with my beloved on whatever path she chooses, to make her way as safe as I can, and to hold her hand every step of the way. I choose you, and in choosing you, I choose love." The king reached for his queen and held her in a tight embrace. He measured his breath to hers and thanked God for their new challenge and all it would bring to their lives.

The old man was buttering a piece of the ground-grain bread freshly baked for his morning meal, when he glanced up to see the king and queen walking toward him. The smell of the freshly baked bread climbed and twisted through the air like spring roses on a fence. "I see that you have made your choice. Good," he said, raising the warm bread to his mouth.

"How can you know without us speaking a word?" asked the queen.

The old man smiled as the bread warmed and filled him. He had learned to not let small pleasures escape him, so he closed his eyes and made himself aware of the moment. Once he had honored the bread with a moment of awareness and appreciation, he raised his face to look upon the queen. "Love can always be seen in the eyes of those who choose it. Love can go where there are no words. It brings to our hearts that which is ineffable. It can be expressed in many ways, shared in many languages, but its essence is obvious in the eyes of those who choose it."

"Then our eyes speak clearly," confirmed the king. "What would you have us do now?"

"Good morn' to you sires, my queen," a young man interrupted. "It is a lovely morning isn't it?" There was no mistaking Pomus's voice. It was raspy and deep like a bottomless well.

The king and queen had taken Pomus to live with them two years earlier when his parents fell ill. Queen Caritas promised her sister that Pomus would be well cared for. The queen felt sadness for his loss, and with great effort convinced the king to give the self-consumed adolescent a position as a royal aid. (The other members of the court were convinced that Pomus, whom they had nicknamed 'Pompous,' had earned a position as a royal something, but as far as they were concerned, it only sounded like aid.) Pomus was prideful, selfish, arrogant, and obstinate, but the queen held some hope that love and kindness might soften the rough edges of his heart.

"And who is this?" Pomus turned to the old man with a slight nod, his dark eyes filled with disdain.

"This is . . ." the king realized that he did not know the old man's name. In all of the conversation, the old man's name had never come up.

Pomus took advantage of the king's gaff. "Forgive the king and queen their rudeness in not learning your name, my good man. Let me introduce myself. I am—"

"You need no introduction;" interrupted the old man, "for who you are speaks more loudly than your words. You are known as Pompous, are you not?"

"Pomus," he spoke distinctly, correcting the old man.

"Forgive me," the old man spoke softly, "I am usually quite

accurate with names." He turned his attention back to the king and queen.

Pomus did not know why, but he took an instant dislike to the old man. "So tell us, old man," he scoffed, "what do people call you?"

"I am known as Corluce, though at another time my name was Tenebre," the old man answered. Then turning, he refocused his gentle eyes on the faces of the royal couple.

"How unusual! What do these names mean?" asked the queen.

"Tenebre means darkness. Corluce means heart light. It took me many years to learn that a name is but a choice. Humans are very different than animals or plants. An elephant can only grow to be an elephant; a horse can only grow to be a horse; and when you plant an acorn, it can only grow to be an oak. Mankind, however, was given the ultimate gift: the gift of choice. We and we alone choose who and what we will grow to be. Who we are is not defined by our birthplace, our name, our color, or our gender. We are ultimately defined by our actions, the value we give to our words, and the meaning that we bring to the lives of others. Take for example your young aid Pompous...I mean Pomus. Your name means fruit tree does it not?" The old man turned once again to Pomus for verification.

Pomus frowned and gave no affirmation.

"Why, yes it does," said the queen.

"And yet, Pomus alone will choose which fruit to bear, or whether to bear fruit at all. It is only his actions, motivations and intentions that can define him. What fruit would you say you presently bear, young Pomus?" asked the old man.

Pomus looked at the old man carefully, studying his face. What trick was hidden in this question? How should he answer in order for him to make the king and queen believe that he was a sincere man? What would he answer in order for the old man to know that he was clever? "I would say—"

"Lemons are particularly sour this time of year," interrupted one of the kitchen maids, "but we have done our best with them. Lemonade, anyone?" She looked past Pomus, and smiled like a child.

"Not now!" snapped Pomus. "Can't you see we are busy?"

"Speaking of names," asked the queen softly, "what shall we name our daughter?"

"What daughter?" questioned Pomus.

"The miracle that is to be ours," answered the queen.

"That's impossible!" he argued.

"All things are possible for those who understand that all things are possible," the old man gently said, focusing his eyes on the light shining in the faces of the royal couple. "You will name her what you see in her eyes the day of her birth. Then she, and only she, will determine by her actions what others call her." The old man turned and gathered his dusty cloak in his arms.

"These are my instructions. Listen with care, though to follow them or not is but for you to decide. I will leave you seeds to plant. I would recommend that you immediately hire a caretaker, someone with experience. The seeds planted now will welcome your daughter's birth with their first blossoms. These seeds have the potential to grow large, strong and beautiful or to fall onto untended soil and die. Their fate, like ours, depends a great deal on how they are cared for. Carefully tended, their roots will reach deep into the earth. As they grow they will remind you and your kingdom that each breath is a gift. They will take in the grief born of the earth, and give back that which is clean, fresh, and clear. Their leaves will be shaped as hearts, and your kingdom will take on a new name. From this day forward your kingdom will be known as Cortellus, which means heartland."

"As you instruct, it will be done," replied the king.

The old man continued, "I also give to you a parchment tied in dipped muslin. You will keep it until the seven are selected one month before your daughter's twenty-first birthday. When the seven select their numbers out of the hundreds that will come for the contest, you will meet with each of them to ask them but one question: 'How do you feel about my daughter's weakness and frailty?'"

"And?" the king asked expectantly.

"You will choose the one who though blind can see, and give to him the parchment," continued the old man, "and on the day before the princess's birthday, all seven men must give the princess the most perfect heart they can find. The princess must choose whose heart belongs to hers."

"This is ridiculous!" interrupted Pomus. "You are not going to take this crazy old man seriously, are you my king? Pomus turned to the old man. "Are you telling them," he raised his voice in frustration, "that their daughter will be very frail and the man who will save her will be blind?"

"We are each blind, for we can only see what we choose to see," the old man replied respectfully. He then reached into his coat and pulled out a pink velveteen bag and a parchment scroll wrapped in dipped muslin. The velveteen bag was square and the size of one of the queen's bed pillows. The bottom third of the bag was full of seeds. The old man placed the bag in the right hand of the king, and the parchment scroll is his left. "The future is in your hands, my good king," he said. "Of course, each of us, whether we are aware of it or not, holds our future in our hands."

A moment later, the old man was gone.

The king turned to Pomus. "Find someone with experience to plant and care for these seeds."

"But sire," Pomus argued, "the old man appears quite mad."

"Do as I command," the king insisted. He handed the pink velveteen bag to his nephew.

"What do I offer the caretaker for his service?" Pomus asked.

"Offer them the small cabin on the east side of the castle. Give them a wagon and tubs to fill with water to care for the seedlings. Tell them they may use the fertile soil between their cabin and the river to grow their food. Give them a cow, three pigs, and hens for laying."

"But that is too much, sire," pleaded Pomus. "I beg you to rethink this."

"Let it be done exactly as I have requested," insisted the king.

As he left the palace, Pomus grumbled angrily under his

breath. "How am I to find a caretaker that has experience with trees?"

He resented doing anything for which he could not foresee any personal benefit, and he certainly did not trust the old man. Of course, Pomus did not trust anyone—including himself.

*W*henever Conoscenzo did not know what to do, he found refuge in his books. This day was no different. He hoped to clear his head by filling it with something other than worry and distress. Once his head was clear, he thought, he might be able to find an answer to the challenges he and his family faced."

Three

The Birth of Faith

Across the city the same morning, a beautiful young woman named Dare awoke on her eighteenth birthday with a distinct sense of excitement and dread. Dare had deep dark eyes and dark skin. Her features were exotic and striking, and her voice was as gentle as her spirit.

The day began with the rays of the sun kissing her awake as they crept like ivy into the small dingy hut. She smiled at the thought of what the day might bring, but then had an unexpected visit from the landlord that owned the small hut in which Dare, her husband, and her parents lived. With an evil smirk he gave them notice of their eviction. Dare pleaded with him to show them mercy, for she was pregnant with her first baby and close to delivery, and her parents were very ill.

"I will show you grace," chided the obese landlord, waving his dusty felt hat in front of her. "I will give you until tomorrow instead of throwing you out today."

As small a grace as this seemed, Dare was grateful, for she believed even the smallest displays of kindness were gifts. Times had been very difficult since Dare's parents fell ill, and what few resources her family had were almost used up. She fought to drive the fear from her mind.

All of a sudden, Dare felt an unfamiliar sensation in her body. *Today?* she questioned. She gently placed her hands on each side of her large stomach. *Are you coming to bring me great joy today?*

A few hours later, Dare gave birth to a beautiful baby boy. Great joy nearly replaced the day's desperation, until the midwife told Dare that because of the complications during her delivery, she would not be able to have more children. She was stunned with grief.

Still, Dare insisted that she would focus on the birth of her beautiful son. *What a miraculous gift,* she thought. *How lucky I am to have it delivered to me on my birthday.*

"Do you still want a rabbit?" Conoscenzo poked his head into the small hut, his warm voice interrupting her thoughts.

"This gift is much better than a rabbit," Dare answered, smiling widely. She lifted her new baby close to her face so she could press her lips gently to his soft cheeks. Conoscenzo had promised Dare a pet rabbit for her birthday. He was relieved that the baby was a far better gift, though, because he did not have the few small coins that it took to buy a rabbit. Dare and Conoscenzo both loved rabbits. They believed that rabbits were the most wonderfully soft things they had ever held, that is until they held their wonderful baby boy.

"Let's name him Coniglio," smiled Dare.

"Coniglio you will be," said Conoscenzo joyously as he lifted his son and held him close to his chest.

Dare looked at Conoscenzo's proud face. He was her heart's delight. They had been married for little over a year, and every day she was reminded why she loved him. She felt beautiful, warm, and deeply loved whenever she was near him. He was tall and slender, with features as sharp as his intellect.

Conoscenzo was a scholar, and his dream had always been to work in a library. To do so, he would have to move to a neighboring kingdom many days' travel from Cortellus, for there was the only library for many miles, and it was a small library at that.

Because Cortellus had a river that bent through the heart of the land and offered a rich and plentiful supply of water, most of the people there were farmers. Much of their lives was spent in the fields, and consequently they had little time for reading.

Conoscenzo had not planned on falling in love with Dare, but when he saw her at the well in the center of the city, his heart could do nothing else. He knew it was love when the first sight of her caused all else to disappear from his vision.

Conoscenzo begged Dare to move away from Cortellus with him, for he could not see himself continuing to live in a kingdom without a wealth of books, but she could not go. Her parents were ill and it was up to her to care for them. She had given her word, and her word held value beyond anything else in her life.

Above all else, Conoscenzo valued books and the words that filled them. If those words had no value, they would not be worth reading. So, Conoscenzo loved Dare all the more for her reverence to her word. They married and he sacrificed his dream to stay with her.

Now they had a son, and Conoscenzo felt greatly troubled. He tried to conceal the fear in his eyes, holding Dare's hand as she and Coniglio fell asleep, both exhausted from the birth. He was supposed to have the answers, but he had none and felt inadequate to be Dare's husband. He was desperate not to fail her, but there had not been enough money to live on before the baby arrived, let alone now. What was he going to do?

Whenever Conoscenzo did not know what to do, he found refuge in his books. This day was no different. He grabbed a book and decided he would take a walk while Dare and the baby slept. He hoped to clear his head by filling it with something other than worry and distress. Once his head was clear, he thought, he might be able to find an answer to the challenges he and his family faced.

Yes," replied the young man, somewhat intimidated by Pomus' arrogant attitude, "Some believe that faith is the poor man's bread."

F_{our}

An Encounter with Destiny

omus had only walked a short distance but was already bored with his search. He was still grumbling to himself about the king and queen's naiveté. *How could they possibly pay attention to an obviously insane old man?* Pomus thought as he rounded a corner near the square and carelessly ran right into a tall, thin man.

"Forgive me, sir," said the thin man as he jumped to his feet quickly, and reached to help Pomus stand up. "I am terribly sorry," he continued as he picked up the pink velveteen bag that Pomus had dropped and dusted it off.

"Don't you look where you are going?" snapped Pomus. He brushed the dust from his uniform.

"Again I ask that you forgive me sir. It was my fault," admitted the man. "I was reading as I walked and was not paying proper attention."

"Certainly it was your fault," Pomus attacked. "What are you reading about that is so important it is worth running down innocent pedestrians?"

"Faith," answered the man.

"It is a book about faith?" questioned Pomus.

"Yes," replied the young man, somewhat intimidated by Pomus' arrogant attitude, "Some believe that faith is the poor man's bread."

"Then let them feast on it," scoffed Pomus. "Faith is for fools. Are you a fool?"

"No sir, simply poor," replied the young man.

Pomus hesitated momentarily. "Do you have any knowledge or experience with plants?"

"No sir. None," answered the man, confused by the strange question.

"How would you like to perform a very important service for the king?" asked Pomus.

"What kind of service?" the young man inquired.

"A service of monumental significance," he answered. "How would you like to be caretaker of the king's new trees? You would be provided with a small cabin to the east of the castle, the land between the cabin and the river to farm, three pigs, a cow, and some hens." Pomus looked away impatiently. "Decide now, or be gone."

"I must be honest," confessed the man. "I know nothing about trees, seeds or plants of any kind. But I would happily accept the job if you could find it in your heart to trust me with it."

This is perfect, Pomus thought. *The old man is crazy. What good are these seeds anyway? Selecting someone who knows nothing about trees increases the odds that these trees will fail. That will show my uncle that the old man is a fool.*

"Come by the castle tomorrow to pick up your wagon and

barrels for water. I will give you the necessary papers you need to move into the cabin and the animals to take with you," Pomus ordered.

"With great pleasure," the man answered.

Pomus began to walk away, then turned. "By the way, what is your name?"

"My name is Conoscenzo, sir. It is my young wife's birthday and the day of my son's birth. You have blessed my family with a great gift. I will never forget your kindness."

"Kindness has nothing to do with it, my good man," Pomus mumbled under his breath.

Conoscenzo ran back to the hut to share his good fortune with his wife. Dare couldn't believe her ears. Once again her tears flowed with joy. "You have saved us my love."

"We have been saved my love, but not by me. Faith and the miracles that accompany it have saved us. What a wonderful beginning for our son to be bathed in faith and miracles," Conoscenzo said, kissing his wife gently on her forehead.

*M*y grandmother says that miracles are born in the hearts of those who believe in them."

Five

The Faint Smile of Dawn

It was a gray day but the light was insistent as it broke through a hole in the dark clouds. The king could not believe that so many months had passed since the old man arrived with his news. He now paced outside the royal suite, his face covered with small beads of perspiration. The screams of his wife broke him like sticks for kindling. Finally one of the midwives came to the door. "Your daughter has arrived and she is beautiful," she said with a smile. The king took the first full breath in the last twenty hours. He had not been aware of how desperate his body was for air until his lungs filled completely. He gasped and wept, overcome with emotion.

"My queen, how is my queen?" he pushed through his tears.

"She is exhausted but well. She wants to see you—but do not stay long, for she must sleep to recapture her strength," cautioned the nurse.

The king rushed to his queen's bed where he found her gently caressing their newborn. Tears were flowing down her face. "Look at your daughter," he whispered. "The princess has arrived." Caritas smiled with pride as she handed the bundle to the king.

"Oh, she is beautiful," he whispered, lost in the miracle.

"What shall we name her?" asked the queen softly, for they

had agreed not to pick a name until they looked into the face of their child.

"Let us name her Alba, for we have always loved the break of day," the king softly suggested.

"Princess Alba it is," smiled the queen. "She will bring light to our lives each day through her love."

The princess was blessed with a kind and sensitive spirit. She was curious, vulnerable, and sparkled like the sunlight she was named for. The king and queen grew more enchanted with her each day, and time passed quickly under her spell.

When Alba was eleven, she was watching the other children run and play, desperately wanting to join them. For years she had listened to the warnings of her caregivers. She knew that her heart was frail and could not hold her as others held them, but she could bear her separation no longer. She lifted herself from her chair in the garden near where she watched the children play and slowly walked toward them.

"Who are you? Are you the princess?" asked the young children, for they had seen her from a distance in the garden.

"Yes," she replied softly.

"Come, run and play with us. Chase us!" they squealed delightedly. They began to run for the princess to pursue.

Princess Alba started to run after them but within a short distance she turned pale. She stopped, clutching her chest, desperate for breath. Everything darkened, and she felt herself falling.

When she regained consciousness she heard the young children mocking her. Fear has a way of causing people to make fun of what frightens them or what they don't understand. All of the children were laughing but one, who had rushed to break her fall when he noticed she was unsteady. He was holding her head gently in his lap.

"Don't listen to them. They are but children," he said as he stroked her dark, silken hair.

"But you are a child too," the princess argued.

"I am not a child," the young man defended, "I am twelve."

"Oh my goodness, that is old," she teased with a smile.

"My grandfather told me that people are only as old as they feel," he continued. "Today I feel quite mature."

"Your grandfather is still alive?" the princess asked, surprised.

"Yes," the boy answered. "It is just one of the many miracles for which my family has been blessed," the young man explained.

"My parents have always told me that I am a miracle," the young princess confessed.

"Then you are," said the young boy. "My grandmother says that miracles are born in the hearts of those who believe in them." His smile matched the one he watched grow shyly on the princess's face. She felt safe in the boy's lap, but then became embarrassed.

"Thank you for your kindness," the princess said, struggling to get up.

"You are welcome. Let me help you," the young man offered respectfully. "I will take you back to your chair if you would like."

"That would be quite nice." The princess wrapped her arms around the young man's neck as he helped her across the garden.

"What is your name?" she asked as they walked slowly.

"My name is Coniglio."

"What an unusual name. What does it mean?" the princess inquired.

"It will embarrass me to tell you," confessed the young man.

"My name is Princess Alba," the princess said. "It means dawn, or the break of day."

"That is a wonderful and fitting name for a princess," Coniglio affirmed.

"Now that I have confessed the meaning of my name," Alba said as the young man helped her position herself comfortably in her chair, "please confess the meaning of yours."

"Mine is not nearly so inspiring, my princess. It is common, even comical."

"Please," the princess pleaded softly.

"It means rabbit. Can you imagine? Rabbit. Not lion, or wolf, or cunning bear, but rabbit."

"Why did your parents name you rabbit?" the princess asked.

"Because it was the softest, gentlest thing that they had ever touched, yet they watched a mother rabbit put herself in front of the path of a fox to save her children. They told me that they wanted me to have a heart that understood the courage of gentleness and sacrifice." Coniglio lowered his head in humiliation. "Men should be strong, keen and powerful. And yet, my parents named me for a mother rabbit."

"I think that it takes the greatest strength to be gentle," said Alba. "It takes greatest courage to be willing to sacrifice your heart for another. To me, my dear rabbit, your parents have done you a great service. Besides, I see you as one of the strongest, keenest, bravest people that I have ever met."

"That is how you see me?" Coniglio asked. He straightened his back and raised his head high. Suddenly he asked, "Do you like to read?"

"I love to read. I love books and knowledge. When you are trapped inside of a body that does not travel well, you must do most of your traveling in your mind. Why do you ask?" she inquired. The princess could not remember feeling this happy in her whole life, but there was something about this conversation, something about the humility and strength of this young man that made her feel better about herself than she had felt before.

"I would love the honor of visiting you each week to read you a book. We will travel the world together, you and I. That is, if the princess is willing to trust me on these adventures…" Coniglio had never wanted anything more than he wanted the princess to say yes.

"I would love that," she said as she smiled with a smile that lit up her heart.

He knew that life is only great moments strung together like a string of pearls and Conoscenzo was committed to not spoiling this one for his son."

Six

Bountiful Blessings

The day was hot and heavy with humidity. The sun because of the time he spent working in the fields and maintaining the Empress trees had browned Conoscenzo's once fair skin. Reaching up to wipe the rolling sweat off his brow, he saw Coniglio running toward him.

"You're late," he called out to Coniglio, who was usually very prompt. Conoscenzo couldn't believe his eyes as he watched his son in his graceful gallop. Could it really have been twelve years ago that he, Dare, her parents, and their new baby boy had moved into the cabin on the east side of the castle? Their lives had felt so rich and blessed since then.

Conoscenzo smiled as he remembered his joy at his first sight of the cabin. It had four small rooms and was double the size of the dingy hut they had lived in previously. The soil next to the river was fertile and rich, the color of chocolate, and Dare and Conoscenzo planted crops immediately. With the eggs and the milk from the cow they were able to make cheese and butter, which had been a rare delicacy previously. To consecrate their new home, they placed the book of faith behind a pane of glass and framed it, to remind them from whom all blessings flow.

Conoscenzo took their new wagon and traveled many days

to the neighboring kingdom, where he traded their new hen eggs for books. The first books that he collected were about horticulture and agriculture. He read each one with care. He then found the perfect spot to plant the first grove of trees. It was a large patch of land next to the river not far from the cabin. There was an abundance of available land in the kingdom of Cortellus, and the king owned most of it.

Conoscenzo took the pink velveteen bag and emptied it into a planting pouch he carried around his neck. He laid the bag next to the river, and in his excitement of planting the first seeds, forgot it. He planted until he could no longer see the seeds, and pleased with his work, walked home by the light of the moon.

Early that next morning a woman and her daughter were on their way to the home of their uncle. The uncle had written them and requested that they come to the country to live with him. This was good since the woman's husband had been killed in war. Although the woman's name was Agninas, which meant lamb, she had the heart of a lion. Not many women would have dared traveled so far alone, especially traveling with her daughter. But Agninas was determined to grant her daughter a chance at something other than becoming a servant. Her daughter's name was Dolce, which meant gentle, and that she was. Agninas and Dolce had stopped at the edge of the river to water their horse before they continued on their journey.

"How much further?" asked Dolce, weary from the ride in the wagon. "That seat is hard as stone," she complained.

"Not far," assured Agninas. "Uncle lives on the outskirts of the kingdom in a small cabin near a well. I have the map he sent us here. It is only a short distance from here. It will be nice there. You will see."

Dolce grabbed the old wooden bucket from the back of the wagon and walked through a small but lovely patch of wild flowers that led to the edge of the river. Dolce loved the flower's bright colors—red, pink, violet, yellow, and blue. It was a beautiful day.

"Be careful not to slip as you near the river's edge," cautioned Agninas.

"Okay," reassured Dolce. Just then her eyes were drawn from the flowers to something equally as bright. "Mama!" Dolce yelled. "Look what I found!" she squealed with delight. "It is so beautiful and soft."

"What is it?" inquired Agninas.

"It looks like an empty bag. It's pink and wonderfully soft. Can I keep it?" pleaded Dolce.

"I don't know," said Agninas. "What if it belongs to someone?"

"They would not have left it here if it belonged to someone who wanted it," Dolce reasoned. "Please, I want it very much. Can't I have it?"

"We will take it with us and decide what to use it for later," Dolce's mother suggested. "For now, maybe you can sit on it. It might help to soften your ride."

"Oh," said Dolce with excitement, "I think that it is much too nice for that. Could you use it to make me a pillow?" pleaded Dolce. "It is so pretty and soft, it would make a wonderful special pillow."

"Your birthday is coming soon. We will see what we can do," smiled Agninas, happy that she had her needles and thread packed in their bundles.

Conoscenzo had learned quickly how to raise and reproduce the Empress trees. He was surprised with how much he loved the land and the trees. He had always thought that books were his only passion, but now there were Dare, Coniglio, the land, and the trees. To Pomus's great dismay, the Empress trees flourished under the care of Conoscenzo.

The trees grew so quickly that Conoscenzo and Dare were able to harvest some of them to make jewelry boxes, small bowls, and spoons to trade for things they needed. The wood was fine hardwood, perfect for small articles, and as the trees grew even larger with each passing year, the wood was used for much larger things. It was beautiful and easy to fashion.

Conoscenzo learned to graft the Empress trees. Because of his knowledge and care, the Empress forests thrived and multiplied. The rich soil next to the river continued to produce a wonderful variety of vegetables, and food was now plentiful. Dare's parents became stronger and stronger, and soon were able to help with the crops and care for the animals. Their lives seemed to be filled with miracles. Each evening Conoscenzo's family looked upon the frame holding the book of faith and counted their blessings. The miracles were as real as the vegetables from their garden. And though they were no longer poor, they continued to hold faith as their daily bread.

Over his twelve young years Coniglio became a voracious reader, which pleased Conoscenzo very much. Coniglio was blessed with the sharp mind of his father and the gentle, loving spirit of his mother. *"How quickly the time has passed,"* thought Conoscenzo as Coniglio ran up to him in the field. Coniglio was out of breath and flushed.

"Father, Father," Coniglio gasped. He was trying to catch his breath and speak at the same time.

"Slow down, son. Why in the world are you so excited, and what has made you late?" asked Conoscenzo.

"They are the same," Coniglio blurted out. "The reason that I am so excited and the reason that I am late."

"Then I am very curious. Tell me your reason," he said. Conoscenzo sensed this was a conversation worth paying attention to. He rested himself on his shovel, and looked into the flushed face of his son.

"I met her," Coniglio said breathlessly.

"Met who?" asked his father.

"The princess—I met her. She was running and suddenly started falling. I caught her, and helped her back to her chair in the garden." Coniglio was smiling bigger than his father had seen in many years.

"And…" prompted his father

"And, she likes me. At least I think that she does. I think that she might like me."

"Yes," his father interrupted, "you keep saying that."

"She wants me to come and read to her every week in the garden. Oh please, Father, I will do anything you ask. I will wake up early; I will do extra work. Please allow me to do this for her," Coniglio pleaded.

"She wants you to read to her?" Conoscenzo attempted to understand fully.

"Well, I guess it would be more correct to say she wants to read together. She loves books, Father. Imagine. She loves books!" he exclaimed. Coniglio felt that his heart was going to beat out of his chest.

"Well, a young woman who loves books must be a fine woman indeed," Conoscenzo said. He reached to ruffle the hair on Coniglio's head. "We will definitely have to insure that the princess has an adequate supply of books, won't we?"

"Oh Father, you are the greatest father in the world! Thank you, sir, thank you," Coniglio said. He grabbed his tools and went to work in the field. Conoscenzo had never seen him so eager to work. He recognized the light in his son's eyes but felt sadness, for he knew that Coniglio had no chance for a future with the princess. Conoscenzo struggled with whether he should explain this to Coniglio, but decided that they would deal with the issue another day. Today, there was too much joy to spoil it with warnings. He would simply let Coniglio have this moment, because he knew that life is only great moments strung together like a string of pearls, and Conoscenzo was committed to not spoiling this one for his son.

ove can always be seen in the eyes of those who choose it. Love can go where there are no words. It brings to our hearts that which is ineffable. It can be expressed in many ways, shared in many languages, but its essence is obvious in the eyes of those who choose it."

Seven

Truth Revealed

he princess sat in her garden as she had hundreds of times before, anxiously waiting for Coniglio, but this time was different. All the other times she waited with a heart filled with joy, but today, her joy was mixed with great angst.

It was twenty-one and a half years ago that Conoscenzo had accepted the job as caretaker of the Empress trees. Over those years, Conoscenzo traveled each month to far-off lands to trade his beautiful wooden products for books, always books, more and more books. He traveled many days just to collect new reading material for Coniglio. And what he brought for Coniglio, Coniglio shared with Princess Alba. Coniglio arrived each week at the garden of the princess to share another book. They studied each book carefully, and Coniglio loved their time together.

They had read over five hundred books together over the years. They would have read more, but Coniglio had to work in the fields and help his parents fashion beautiful wood products. With his father's full support, though, he made special time each week just for reading. He and the princess read books of philosophy, astronomy, religion, finance, crafts, medicine, painting, sculpture, poetry, love stories, and life stories. They read children's books, fables, mysteries, and war strategies. They read science books and math books, and love sonnets by great masters of the times. They had traveled the world together over the last ten years, and each book opened their eyes more widely to the great and limitless possibilities in the world.

As Coniglio entered the garden, his smile widened when he saw the princess. He held up the new book as he walked toward her. It was hard for her to believe that he was the young man who had broken her fall nine years previously. Coniglio was now twenty-one. He was tall, strong, and handsome. His eyes were bright and alive, and his passion for continual learning was inspiring. His thirst for knowledge and his gentle spirit were the two things Alba loved most about him. *How am going to tell him?* she thought anxiously. Today was the day; she knew that she could put it off no longer. Time was closing in on her, and she would also be turning twenty-one sooner than she cared to imagine. It did not matter to her that she might die. Dying would be easier than the thought of living without Coniglio.

The contest was near. She knew that she was to marry the man that might save her, and together they would rule the kingdom, but how could she marry anyone but Coniglio? He was her love. The sight of him kept her heart beating.

"What's wrong, Alba?" Coniglio interrupted the princess's thoughts.

"What do you mean?" she asked, knowing that it was impossible for her to hide her true nature from her beloved.

"You know exactly what I mean," he insisted. "Is it your heart? Are you weary? Are you in pain?"

"No, no, I'm fine, really I am," the princess replied.

"Then what? Your face is tense and strained, empty of joy. You do not look like yourself," Coniglio said. His fingers brushed her hair from her eyes.

"I must tell you something, Coniglio. It is something that will be almost impossible to understand, but you need to know," confessed the princess.

"Alright. Tell me. I'm quite good at impossible things. I try to do at least six impossible things before breakfast each day," Coniglio said and laughed, attempting to ease the burden on the princess's heart.

"Sit here next to me and I will tell you the whole story. It is a tragic tale, and sadly it is my tragic tale." The princess then told him the full story, from the beginning.

"What are you saying?" asked Coniglio.

"I am saying that there is going to be a contest. Seven will be selected from the hundreds of contestants that enter. One of them will offer to me a heart of perfection that will heal me, or I will die on my twenty-first birthday," said the princess, her eyes filling with tears.

"Then the perfect heart you must have," said Coniglio, shocked by the story his princess had told.

"But without you I will die anyway," the princess said, now weeping. Coniglio was stunned. He had been in love with the princess since the moment he broke her fall, but he never imagined that she could feel the same about him. In all of the years they had been reading and sharing, she had never told him of her love.

"Why have you never spoken of this before?" Coniglio asked.

"Because the old man who brought news of me to my parents said that love can always be seen in the eyes of those who choose it. Love can go where there are no words. It brings to our hearts that which is ineffable. It can be expressed in many ways, shared in many languages, but its essence is obvious in the eyes of those who choose it. Have you never seen it in my eyes?" asked the princess.

"I must confess," said Coniglio. "I have seen it many times but would not, and could not, allow myself to believe it. I am just a common man. You are a princess. I knew that someday you would have to choose someone whose status was more fitting for a princess.

"Now you know that I must pick one of the seven. I have no other options. I need for you to select a number in the contest," the princess said, weeping as she pulled Coniglio close. "Please, you must join the contest."

"I cannot. I have no perfect heart to heal you. Besides, what are the chances that I would draw one of the seven numbers?" Coniglio argued.

"What of miracles, Coniglio? What of faith? You must draw a number for me. You must! I beg you." The princess began to cough. She grabbed her chest and struggled to catch her breath.

"Help me, someone help me," called Coniglio. He felt helpless. He reached for the princess and once again kept her from falling. "Don't worry, Alba, I will do what you ask, for I haven't the will to break your heart, and I cannot bear to see you in pain. Relax and breathe deeply, my sweet princess. I will always be here to catch you," reassured Coniglio.

*hoose the one,
who though he is
blind, can see."*

Eight

The Seven Contestants

The king, still lost in thought, turned his eyes upward. He lifted his fingers to his lips where he placed a kiss, and like a child with bubbles blew it toward heaven. "Caritas," the king started to whisper, "I—"

Pomus cleared his throat. "Sorry to interrupt, sire," he said unapologetically, "the time is here."

It had been twenty-five years since Pomus had come to live in the castle, and his heart had not softened at all. Pomus believed that because he was related to the king, and because the princess was so frail, the throne should and would soon be his. "I do not know why you insist on going through with this ridiculous charade, sire," he admonished. "This whole contest idea is an embarrassment to your great intellect. Please reconsider."

"I must do what I must do, Pomus. You know that I must," the king insisted. "The old man left explicit instructions."

"The old man? The old man was crazy," Pomus maintained. "With all due respect, sire, I beg you to reconsider what you are about to do. I know that you are concerned about the princess, but although she is frail, she seems stable. How do you know that what the old man predicted has any merit?"

"How I know that it does *not* is the more important question to be considered here. If I do not follow the old man's instructions, Alba might die," the king said wearily. He had lost his energy for argument. "I have nothing to lose and much to gain."

"You have your reputation and your good name as a sane and intelligent king, sire. The people think that what you are about to do is craziness, and frankly, I must agree with them." Pomus stepped close the king and helped him to stand.

"Have you ever loved anyone Pomus, truly loved them?" the king asked.

"Why yes, sire. I love you and the princess, and I loved Queen Caritas," Pomus answered. The truth was, though, that he had never loved anyone other than himself.

"Then you must understand what I must do," the king said, walking slowly to his throne room.

He called for the contestants to be brought before him, one by one. Of course, he was aware that not one of the seven was blind. The king struggled to get comfortable in his seat. He held the parchment, still wrapped in the original dipped muslin, in his hand. For twenty-one years he had kept it safe for this day.

"I am ready," the king stated with tenuous calm. He was squeezing the parchment, so he laid it gently to his side and took a long deep breath. *Choose the one, who though he is blind, can see.* The words raced through his mind.

The first contestant to enter the throne room was a prince from a far-off land. He was tall and strong, both in body and will. His dominating height and the breadth of his chest demanded attention. His rigid belief system expressed itself in his body and voice. His head was wrapped in a multicolored turban and his dark eyes danced with delight as he fantasized about winning the throne of Cortellus.

It had been carefully explained to the prince upon joining the contest that the princess was to become queen and rule her people if her heart was restored, but this prince believed that once he was married to her he could change and control her will, making her understand her proper role.

There had never been a woman who ruled the land from which he had journeyed, and he was sure that any land would surely fall if the leader was as frail and gentle as this princess was. He intended to do her a great service and remove the burden that was not meant to be hers and put it on the back of a capable, strong, willful warrior—where such burdens had always belonged. He knew that his way was the only right way.

The prince stepped toward the king, and slapped his wrist to his strong armored chest as he straightened his body and dropped his head in respect of the king.

"I have but one question, my strong prince. How do you feel about the princess's weakness and frailty?" the king asked.

The prince spread his legs and placed his strong arms behind his back. "The princess needs the heart of a warrior to defend and protect her, sire. I am a great warrior. When people look upon her weakness and frailty, they will see my strength instead and back away. And if they do not, I will blind them, so that they can see no more."

"Thank you, my fine warrior," the king said. "You may be excused." The prince once again slapped his wrist to his chest, turned in one quick motion, and left. "Bring to me the man who drew the number two," said the king.

The second man was known throughout the land as the finest jeweler in Cortellus. He was usually on edge because of the jewels that he would transfer from his shop to his safe at home. But his jewels were not the only things he guarded well. He guarded himself. He was afraid that if people knew more of him than his clothes, his jewels, and his talents, they might discover that he was flawed and therefore unworthy of love and respect.

The jeweler was thin with short dark curly hair. His face was pleasing and his clothes were as carefully selected as the stones in his jewelry. Anyone who saw the jeweler had to confess that his taste was impeccable.

No one knew where the jeweler came from originally. Only he knew that he had grown up very poor. The cruel teasing and taunting he had received as a child had wounded his heart. His constant sense of being flawed and unworthy pushed him unmercifully toward success. He had vowed that once free from the taunting and poverty of his childhood he would never be teased again. He vowed to never be seen unless perfectly groomed.

"I have but one question, my fine jeweler. How do you feel about the princess's weakness and frailty?" the king asked for the second time.

"I am a jeweler, sire," he said. "I know how to create magnificent jewelry for the princess that will blind others to her vast weaknesses. I will drape the princess with my creations, so that the jewels will distract all. I will help her to hide that which is weak and frail," answered the jeweler nervously.

The king was puzzled. Here was the second man to talk of blinding others to his daughter's frailty. He hoped that the next contestants would be better and he would not have to choose between these first two.

"Thank you," the king said. "Now bring to me the man who drew the number three," said the king.

The third contestant entered the room. His hair was long, sandy in color, with curls that fell to his shoulders. His face was weathered, but pleasing, and his features were strong and sharp, while his eyes were soft and warm. The man wore long and beautiful robes. He had traveled an incredible distance—some said he came from the Orient—for he longed to leave a great legacy that would linger long after his death, and he believed that winning the heart of the princess would help him do just that.

"I have but one question, tall traveler. How do you feel about the princess's weakness and frailty?" the king asked for the third time.

"Weakness and frailty are likened to the soft petals of a rose. It is the rose's petals that blind people to its thorns. They are weak and frail but fragrant and lovely. The thorns are strong and protective but without beauty. I would act as the princess's thorns. I would protect her delicate petals from the harshness of the world."

The king was confused by the man's seemingly poetic nature. *I am not sure that I know what he means,* the king thought. "Thank you for your answer, you may be excused," he said. As the man exited the throne room, the king could not help but remember the day that Alba was born. What a gift she had been these twenty years. Yes, there had been many struggles with her health, but the joy she brought to his life had been immeasurable. These men that he interviewed were all strangers. He wrestled with what he was doing. How could the old man, who seemed so kind, leave this fate for his daughter? *None of this makes sense,* the king thought.

"The fourth contestant is waiting, sire," Pomus once again interrupted. "Would you like to end this ridiculous contest now, or would you like me to bring him in?"

"Bring him to me," answered the king.

The next to enter the throne room was a stout, squatty man. He was an artist, well known and well loved for his fine work. He had a large mustache that curled at the ends. He was dressed in bright, multi-colored clothing trimmed in various beads and tassels, and although he may have resembled a clown in color, his countenance was quite serious in nature. He carried himself with solemn passion. As he approached the steps of the throne, he bowed dramatically for the king. The king would have laughed except for the serious look on the artist's face.

"I have but one question, my fine artist. How do you feel about the princess's weakness and frailty?" the king asked. This was the fourth time he had asked the question and he still had not gained clarity about what to do with the scroll.

"The princess can be likened to a beautiful canvas painted with weakness and frailty. I will repaint her and redefine her. I will paint the most wonderful portraits of her highness and have them hung all throughout the kingdom. In that way people will see the princess without her frailties. The paintings will create a vision of her that the kingdom will see, and only we in the castle will know the truth. In this way the princess will be protected."

"Thank you, my fine artist. That is all I need of you today." The king was growing anxious. "Bring me the fifth contestant," he said.

The fifth man was the banker of the land. He was short, round, and balding, and his eyes would have appeared blue if you could see them through the slits in his pudgy face. He was a mathematical genius and was considered one of the finest minds in the land with regard to finances and investments. He had amassed a large fortune and had great financial wealth but was hungry for the power that could only be his by marrying the princess.

"I have but one question, my fine banker. How do you feel about the princess's weakness and frailty?" the king asked for the fifth time.

"Weakness and frailty are easily covered by wealth. I will dress the princess in the finest of fashions. No one will ever see her in the same gown twice. I will surround her with the best that money can buy. I will have her carried on a gilt throne throughout the kingdom by the strongest and most handsome men. She will be so well taken care of that her weakness and frailty will not show."

"Thank you," said the king. He was growing more weary and anxious by the minute. "Bring me the sixth contestant," he said without animation.

The sixth man had thick, black hair pulled tightly behind his head. He walked quietly, as though his feet did not touch the floor, and stood quietly, calling little attention to himself. He guarded himself, but differently than the jeweler. This man had been trained as a warrior but did not have the heart for it. Longing to celebrate all that lived, he could not allow himself to cause the end of a life. His father was disgraced by the young man's choice, so the young man had traveled to Cortellus hoping to create a new beginning.

"I have but one question, my fine traveler," the king said. "How do you feel about the princess's weakness and frailty?"

"I believe that weakness and frailty are but illusions, so I see the princess's weakness as an illusion of this world. I will drape it and cloak it in more illusion. No one will know if it is real. No one will be able to believe his or her eyes. They will question if the princess was ever frail in the first place," the man spoke, in a voice that seemed to come from everywhere and nowhere.

"Thank you, fine traveler," the king said, trying to make sense of what he just saw, or did not see. Had the old man been talking about illusion? Was that what he meant by blindness? The king was getting quite anxious. He had but one more contestant to interview. Who was he to give the parchment to? His hands were wet with perspiration, his chest tight with worry. "Bring to me the man who drew the number seven," said the king.

The king was speechless when he looked upon the face of the seventh man. "Coniglio, what are you doing here?" he asked, greatly surprised.

"I am the man who drew the seventh number, sire."

"I did not know that you were a contestant," said the king.

"The princess told me that it would break her heart if I refused to draw. I tried to reason with her, my king. I explained that the number should be left to someone more fit than I was to save her. But she said that her heart would break completely unless I agreed to draw; and sire, only you could understand that I did not have a choice. Under no circumstance could I burden the heart of Princess Alba."

"But what of her heart? She must receive the perfect heart in order to live. How do you intend to offer such a heart?"

"I have spent many months crafting a magnificent heart box from the wood of the Empress trees. They have added so much to our land and they symbolize all that is strong and noble about us. I have carefully carved, smoothed and painted every piece of the box. I have inlaid it with delicate designs. I have lined the inside with rabbit fur."

"Rabbit fur?" the king interrupted.

"Yes sire." Coniglio smiled. *Rabbit fur, how the princess will love that,* he thought.

"Rabbit fur is as soft as the heart of a princess, and a symbol of good fortune and miracles. Inside the box I have placed written words from my heart. They express my deepest sentiments for the princess. They are honest and sincere. The wood of the Empress trees symbolizes the richness of soil that in many ways is the heart of Cortellus. The box is hand rubbed with stain from vegetables I grew myself. I began crafting the heart box when I gave my promise to enter the contest to the princess. At first, I thought that I had nothing to offer the heart of a princess but I am pleased with the box, for it represents the meaning of my words."

Coniglio reached into his jacket and pulled out an exquisite box. "It is done, and I am ready to give my very best to the princess," he said with great commitment. "I love her, sire. I would give all that I have to her, including my life."

"I have no doubt that your heart is in the right place, young man for you have been more faithful to the princess than anyone. If love has anything to do with all of this, then there is no question. Yours is true. It was with love that this all began twenty-one years ago. Let us pray that it is with love that it will end. Now I must ask you one question. How do you feel about the princess's weakness and frailty?" asked the king for the last time.

"I don't know," answered Coniglio.

"You don't know? What do you mean you don't know?" replied the king.

"I don't know how to answer your question, sire," continued Coniglio.

"And why in heaven's name not?" he asked, amazed. This only proved that Coniglio should not have drawn a number. What if he had taken the place of the blind man? What if he was risking the princess's life with his wooden heart? He could not even answer the simplest of questions.

"I don't know how to answer your question, sire," Coniglio continued, "because I don't know the weakness and frailty of which you speak. I have known the princess for a very long time and in that time I have seen only grace and wisdom in her. I have witnessed a strength and a courage that can be seen in very few. Her beauty, her gentle nature, and her compassion have awed me. Frailty and weakness are not what I see when I look at the princess, so I cannot answer as to how I might feel about them."

Oh great glory to Goodness, thought the king. *This is a man, though he is blind to the princess's weakness and frailty, can see her beauty, strength, wisdom and courage.*

"You have made me extremely happy this day, Coniglio. Come close to me," the king instructed.

Coniglio stepped close to the king. He wasn't sure of what he had done to make the king so pleased.

"Take this; it belongs to you." The king handed Coniglio the scroll wrapped in dipped muslin. "It was left for you many years ago. No one's eyes have looked upon its contents. Go now and look upon it," he said.

The king was no longer exhausted. Maybe the heart-shaped box made from the Empress trees was the perfect heart for the princess. After all, it was the old man who had left the seeds in the first place. Maybe all this was a puzzle that the young Coniglio had accidentally figured out. How wonderful it would be if after all of this time, the seeds brought the princess the healing she needed.

Coniglio was confused and excited as he left the throne room. He didn't really care about the parchment. To him it was simply an old piece of paper. All he could think about was how glad he was that the king was pleased with his special heart. He believed that if it was good enough to please a king, it was probably good enough for the princess.

Just outside, Pomus was watching and listening through the crack in the throne room door. *I must destroy that box,* he thought. He did not believe the old man's prediction. He had no faith in the princess's healing, or the possibility that she might die on her next birthday. He did not want the princess to die, either; he simply wanted the throne for himself.

As Coniglio was leaving, Pomus stepped in front of him. He eyed the box Coniglio was clutching with pride. "Beautiful box," he said. "Where did you get it?"

"I made it. It was a labor of love. Do you like it?" Coniglio asked innocently.

"It is the most beautiful I have seen," reassured Pomus, as he noticed the parchment scroll leaning out of Coniglio's pocket.

"I have to go, Pomus. I have to tell my family that the king loved the box. Imagine! The king loved the box." Coniglio felt as though he had wings and could fly home.

As Coniglio turned to rush away, the parchment spun out of his pocket and landed on the granite floor in front of Pomus. Pomus could not believe his eyes or his good fortune. It appeared that fate was smiling on him. He rushed to his room, where he hid the parchment under his down mattress. All that was left in order to insure his place on the throne was to destroy the box. He began plotting.

our fruit, the fruit that
you produce for others
to share, defines you."

Nine

Love is the Brightest Fire

The light of dawn was welcoming the morning as Pomus stood on the dew-soaked grass, hiding in a grove of small trees just west of the cabin. He had watched Coniglio and his family for a few days, trying to get a sense of their daily routines. He knew that Conoscenzo and Coniglio left each morning to care for the trees and that Dare and her parents went to the fields. They loved working in the rich soil and caring for the gardens.

Pomus was desperate to destroy the beautiful wooden box made of the wood of the Empress trees. He knew that the princess loved Coniglio, but he needed control of the throne. Once he was in charge, Coniglio could fashion all the beautiful heart boxes he wanted in hopes of healing the princess, but by then it would be too late for her to become queen.

Pomus had his plan. This morning when the family left the cabin, Pomus would pour a fuel used for burning around the cabin. The family left as expected. Pomus snuck into the cabin, poured fuel all over the floor, and lit it. The fire started quickly, and Pomus rushed out, hiding once again in the small grove of trees. Smoke began to rise from the cabin.

Conoscenzo had forgotten the cheese and bread that Dare set out for him each morning. He was on his way home to collect it when he saw the cabin in flames. He was frantic. To Pomus's surprise, Conoscenzo ran into the cabin. Pomus ran in after him, for he meant for no one to be harmed. As he entered the cabin a large beam fell over him.

Conoscenzo was grabbing the framed book off the wall. When he saw Pomus, he ran quickly to help him.

"Leave me, you crazy fool," Pomus screamed at Conoscenzo.

Conoscenzo forced the frame into one of Pomus's hands and strained to lift the beam off of him. "It seems that each time we meet, you are calling me a fool," he said. The fire was burning faster now. Smoke clouded up the room.

"Leave me! Save yourself," Pomus cried.

"How could I leave you, when your bravery and caring brought you here to save me? What kind of life would that leave me?" Conoscenzo asked, continuing to struggle with the beam.

"You are going to die. Don't be a fool!" Pomus screamed.

"It is better to die bravely for a just cause." Coughing, Conoscenzo stepped back into the flames and reemerged with a small beam. He placed it under the large beam that trapped Pomus. "Leverage," he quipped, coughing again as he continued to work.

Pomus was stunned by the giant will of such a willowy man. In a moment he had moved the beam enough for Pomus to pull himself from under it. The room was too smoky to see much now. Pomus felt around for Conoscenzo, who had fallen, his lungs taken by the smoke. With all of his strength, Pomus grabbed Conoscenzo and pulled him outside.

Conoscenzo was limp. He struggled for breath, reaching for Pomus's coat. Pomus pulled Conoscenzo close to him. He couldn't remember ever having anyone this close to his heart. "How can you ever forgive me?" Pomus cried.

"You have given my family much." Conoscenzo fought to speak. Pomus leaned closer to hear him. "Your trust and faith have blessed us in many ways. We can never repay you. You are a great man, Pomus, with a great heart, and any forgiveness you believe that you might need from me, is yours."

"You're a fool. That's what you are, a fool!" Pomus bawled.

"A fool for faith…a fool for love…a fool for miracles—yes, you could have been right about me all this time, Pomus," Conoscenzo coughed, gasping for air. "Tell my family that I love them, now and forever," he paused, "and that my last words were words of love." His eyes were wet with tears. "Dare loves words. Tell her, will you? I will be forever indebted—"

With that, Conoscenzo struggled no more. Pomus held Conoscenzo for the next hour, until he heard the family returning from the river. When Dare saw that the cabin was in ashes, she began running towards Pomus.

"Oh my God! What happened?" she cried breathlessly.

"He died while trying to save my life," Pomus said. It was all he could speak through his tears. "I ran in to save him, but I was trapped under a beam. He lifted the beam from me, but the smoke overtook his lungs. I pulled him out but it was too late." Pomus continued to weep softly. "I was too late."

"There, there, Pomus. He did what he had to do," Dare said, still in shock.

"But he was so slender and weak. What made him think that he could do such a thing? He was not born to lift large beams," Pomus insisted.

"Conoscenzo often said that humans are very different than animals or plants. We have been given the gift of choice. We are ultimately defined by our actions, the value we give to our words, and the meaning that we bring to the lives of others. We and we alone choose who and what we will grow to be." She began to cry.

Where have I heard that? wondered Pomus. Then he remembered the words of the old man. Pomus struggled to remember the words that had followed. *What is the fruit that you have chosen to bear?* Pomus looked at the still face of Conoscenzo. "This cannot be the fruit that I have chosen to bear," he whispered.

"He is gone," Dare said, bewildered. "Conoscenzo is gone. But I thank you, Pomus, for doing all that you could do for him." Her compassion cut Pomus like the blade of a sharp-ened bread knife.

"I have never done all that I could do for anyone," he con-fessed through his distress. "I have been selfish. It has always been about me and only me," he cried, pulling Conoscenzo to him.

"He saw you much differently than that," Dare explained. She gently pulled the hair from her beloved's face. "In his eyes, you were a miracle, a man of goodness, grace, generosity, and valor. Each night we prayed, we would include you among those things for which we were grateful."

"I am none of those things. You are wrong about me," Pomus said quietly.

"Maybe it is you who are wrong about your vision of yourself. Your fruit, the fruit that you produce for others to share, defines you. You have shared rich, delicious fruit with us," Dare said, touching his arm. "My husband believed you were worth giving his life for. That is proof of your greatness; it is proof enough for me."

Dare's parents were now beside her. She gently pulled Conoscenzo from the lap of Pomus and placed him carefully on her own. As Pomus stood up, the framed book on faith fell from his coat where he had shoved it during the fire. He caught it before it hit the ground.

"This is what your husband went into the burning cabin to rescue," Pomus said softly, handing the framed book to Dare.

"Sentimental man," Dare smiled sadly as she reached to wipe the tears. "He has another just like it, you know. The king allows him to store his books, hundreds of them, in an unused room at the bottom of the castle." Her body felt limp and weak, and the tears fell freely, landing on the glass.

"Then why go back for this one?" Pomus asked, confused.

Dare looked up, her wet eyes fixed on Pomus's face. "This is the book that he was reading when he first ran into you on the most desperate and hopeless day of our lives. It was the day you made him caretaker of the Empress trees. He believed that this book had the power to change the direction of lives, because his reading of it changed the direction of ours."

A chill ran through Pomus. He remembered clearly how he had run into Conoscenzo as he rounded the corner. He was astonished that his hasty choice on that day so long ago had created the most significant opportunity in Dare's and Conoscenza's lives. He watched in bewilderment as Dare turned the frame over and loosened the small nails that held the glass in the frame.

"His belief in this book inspired his life," she said softly as she handed the book to Pomus. "His belief in you inspired him to risk his life to save yours. I believe that Conoscenzo would want you to have this. He valued his books above all else—that is, all else but love."

Pomus did not want the book but he could not refuse Dare's kindness. "I will send the king's men tomorrow to rebuild your cabin. Coniglio will be returning soon. When he arrives, I want you and your family to come to the castle, where you will stay until your home is rebuilt," Pomus said.

"Your generosity continues to be a blessing," Dare said.

Pomus headed back to the castle alone. He had never known heartache like this. When he had lost his parents, he pushed the pain away, pretending that it was just life playing its mean and selfish games. He had promised himself that he would never be hurt again because he would never care about anyone but himself. But now the pain in his heart was overwhelming. It was not life's mean games that caused this tragedy, but his own selfishness.

Pomus walked into his room and sat down on his bed, dazed. How could he repay Dare and her family for this horrible tragedy he caused? What was he to do now that he had caused so much unnecessary pain and grief? Exhausted by the terrifying and tragic events of the day, he laid his head down. When it hit the pillow, he remembered the parchment.

ook what it says on the map:
Where your heart is, there
shall your treasure be also."

Ten

The Treasure

The next morning, Pomus opened the book of faith and read it in its entirety. The book was about a man who, like Conoscenzo, believed in miracles and gave his life for the benefit of others. This morning, a new light of grace seemed to be dawning on Pomus, and if there was ever a time he needed it, it was now.

He reached under his mattress and found the parchment. He had not taken the time to open it in his haste to destroy Coniglio's wooden heart box, and now he did not care what it said. He ran to guest rooms where he knew Coniglio and his family were staying.

"Coniglio. Coniglio!" Pomus yelled, pounding on the large wooden door of the room. "Wake up! I have found something that belongs to you."

Coniglio came to the door half awake. He had not slept through the night, and his eyes were swollen from crying. "What is it, Pomus? What in the world are you yelling about?"

"The parchment that the king gave you—I found it on the floor where you must have dropped it," he said. Pomus shoved the parchment into Coniglio's hands.

"I don't care about any of this anymore," Coniglio said. "My box has gone up in flames, my father is dead, and the heart in my chest is too broken to care."

"You must at least look at it, Coniglio. What if it is important?" Pomus insisted.

"You open it and tell me what it says," insisted Coniglio. He shoved the parchment back into Pomus's hands.

"Alright, I will open it," Pomus said. He carefully removed the dipped muslin from around the parchment. He unrolled the parchment, and to his surprise there was a map of the hills at the edge of the kingdom.

"Well, what is it?" asked Coniglio.

"It looks like a treasure map," answered Pomus, turning the parchment to get his proper bearings.

"What makes you think that?" asked Coniglio, wearily.

"Because it says, *"Where your heart is, there shall your treasure be also.* And look—there is an X. Something must be buried there. We should go and look," suggested Pomus.

"I am in no mood for seeking," confessed Coniglio. "I am lost and exhausted."

"What better time to seek than when you are lost?" recommended Pomus. "Now, it will take us two full days to ride there, and two full days to return. The contest is only five days away, so we must hurry. This map could be very important. It might have something to do with the princess," Pomus suggested.

"The princess," said Coniglio. "What about the princess? I have no worthy heart to give her, no way to save her."

"If we found some treasure, that might help," suggested Pomus.

"There is no time," snapped Coniglio.

"Not if you keep arguing with me there isn't. We must leave immediately," insisted Pomus.

"You are right, Pomus. It is worth a try." Coniglio said, reaching for his clothes. "Get the horses ready. I will meet you in the courtyard. I must tell my family where I am going; now is not the time to have them worried."

"As you wish," Pomus said. He left Coniglio feeling hopeful. Maybe by helping Coniglio to find this treasure, he could begin to atone for the selfishness that cost Coniglio's family so much.

The two men rode as hard as they could through the meadowlands and the forest of prickly pines, into the mountains drawn on the map. After two full days of riding, they found the large rock described on the map at the base of the mountain.

"This is it!" Pomus exclaimed. "This is the rock on the map."

"Yes, I think you are right," Coniglio said.

They began digging with the shovels they had carried from the castle. For hours they dug all around the base of the rock and found nothing. They were exhausted from the heat of the day and the digging.

"It's no use," said Coniglio throwing his shovel to the ground. "This is a waste of time."

"Have faith, Coniglio." Pomus stopped. He couldn't believe those words had come from inside of him. He looked around once more, this time carefully observing all that was around him. As he glanced up, he saw a flat ledge on the rock. A strange bush seemed to be growing out of the rock. "How can that be?" Pomus asked. "Bushes cannot grow out of rock." He looked more closely. "Coniglio!" he exclaimed, "That bush is shaped like a heart. Look what it says on the map: *Where your heart is, there shall your treasure be also.*"

Coniglio picked up his shovel and climbed slippery slope to the ledge. The bush was growing out of a hole in the rock. Coniglio dug around the back of the bush and loosened the soil with his shovel. As he continued to dig deeper, his shovel hit something solid. "I found something," Coniglio yelled down to Pomus. Coniglio scraped the dirt away from a thick canvas bag and pulled it out of the soil. "It's a bag," he said.

"What is inside of it?" Pomus yelled.

Coniglio slowly opened the bag. Inside was a magnificent gold box. It was small, square, and intricately carved. "A gold box," Coniglio whispered, lost in its beauty, and the surprise of finding it.

"Well," urged Pomus. "What did you find?"

Coniglio lifted the clasp to the box and slowly opened its lid. He gasped in complete awe at what he saw.

"What is it? What is it?" hounded Pomus impatiently.

"It's...beautiful." It was all Coniglio could speak, for the treasure's beauty was impossible to describe.

"Coniglio, tell me what you found!" Pomus yelled. He was starting to climb the rock, for his anxiety and curiosity were beginning to get the better of him.

"I am coming, Pomus. Relax. I will be down in a minute," Coniglio said. He placed the box carefully in his vest pocket. Climbing down slowly, he tried to make sense out of all that had happened in the recent weeks. None of it made any sense, especially this.

"Let me see it. Let me see it," Pomus said excitedly.

Coniglio reached into his pocket and pulled out the box. He held it in his open palm, still awed and confused.

Pomus reached for the box and carefully opened it. He began to weep. It was the proof he needed for faith. Pomus closed the box, and with tears from deep within him cascading down his face, handed it back to Coniglio.

"I could never have discovered this without you, Pomus," Coniglio said as he also began to weep.

"And I could never have discovered my treasure if it were not for you and your father, Coniglio," Pomus replied. "This map was as much for me as it was for you."

"I don't understand," said Coniglio.

"Where your heart is, there shall your treasure be also," Pomus said. "I finally know who I am and what I am supposed to do. I must leave now, Coniglio. Can you make it back to castle on your own?"

"Yes, of course, but where are you going?" Coniglio asked.

"I am taking this book," Pomus pulled the book of faith out

of his jacket, "and I am going to share its good news with others," Pomus said. "I have chosen the fruit that I will be defined by. It is the fruit your father grafted to my branches with his faith in me."

"But where will you go?" asked Coniglio.

"Where I am led," Pomus answered, "for like a man who is blind, I will trust my path to He who loves me."

Pomus grabbed Coniglio and hugged him. He felt the spirit of Conoscenzo within both of them. Then, turning, he tied the shovel to a pouch on his saddle.

"What's in the pouch?" asked Coniglio, noticing it for the first time.

"Seeds," Pomus answered as he mounted his horse. "By the way, Coniglio, the last words of your father were of forgiveness, appreciation and grace. He wanted you and your mother to know that. They were his last earthly gifts to you," Pomus said.

"Thank you," said Coniglio. "I will share this with my mother. I am sure that she will find great comfort in it. That sounds like my father, to leave his love in the gift of his words."

"What shall I tell the princess?" Coniglio asked as Pomus turned his horse to leave.

"Tell her that I love her and that I have faith that her heart will be healed. Ask her to name her first son Anthony after me," Pomus said with a smile.

"After you? Your name is Pomus," he said. "I don't understand."

"You will," Pomus said, and with that, he rode away.

*T*here, holding Optare, she sat silently and listened as Coniglio cried. Her grandmother had told her once that sometimes the best thing that you can do when someone is very sad is sit quietly and listen to what their hearts say as they cry. So she did."

Eleven

Finding Hope

oniglio, tired from his long ride back from the mountains, was nearing the well on the outskirts of the kingdom. He had been thinking all morning of how sweet the cool water was going to taste. His horse was thirsty and tired too so he slowed him to a gentle walk. Coniglio took the box from his vest pocket, and opened it slowly. Each time he saw it, the sight of the treasure took his breath. He couldn't wait to see the princess's face when she saw it for the first time. His thoughts were interrupted by the voice of a young girl.

"What are you staring at?" The girl was standing next to the well.

Coniglio closed the box and quickly slid it back into his vest pocket. "Who are you?" he asked.

"My name is Speranza, but people call me Spes," said a small voice through sobs and tears.

"What's wrong? Why are you crying, Speranza?" Coniglio asked, sliding down from his horse.

"My grandmother died," Spes pushed out between sobs," and now I am all alone. I was thirsty. I wanted a drink. I reached for the rope and my dolly Optare fell in the well."

Coniglio looked over the edge of the well and saw the doll.

It was stuffed cloth and its body was lying bent in half, limp across on of the ropes low in the well. "I see her," he said without thinking.

"You see her!" Spes leaped with joy. "Can you get her for me?" she begged.

"I don't know; she is pretty far down there," Coniglio answered cautiously. He did not want to cause the little girl more pain.

"Please, you must save her. She is the only one that I have left. All the rest of my family has gone to heaven. She is the only one left. Please!" the little girl pleaded. She started to sob again.

"There, there, don't cry," said Coniglio as he brushed Spes's long blonde curls from her face. He couldn't help but feel sorry for her. She was small, with big blue eyes filled with tears. Her cheeks were flushed and red from crying.

Coniglio turned back to the well and reached for the rope on which the doll was caught. As he began to pull it, the doll teetered. He knew that if he tried to lift up the rope that it was caught on, the doll would probably fall. Coniglio spotted another rope on the other side. If he could lower himself into the well using that rope, he might safely rescue the doll. He climbed over the edge of the well, and with great care slid down inch by inch into the well. He was just about to grab the doll when the robe that was holding him gave way. His body began to fall. He grabbed for the doll with one hand and the rope she was caught on with the other. The force flipped him upside down. His foot caught in the rope and helped stabilize his weight.

At that very moment, Coniglio had the most horrible sensation. Time stood still as he watched the gold box fall from his vest pocket. He looked at the doll. If he dropped it, he might be able to catch the box. He couldn't break the heart of the child so there was nothing he could do but to watch the gold box, and the treasure within it, disappear into the darkness.

Coniglio slowly made his way out of the well and handed the doll to Spes. He fell lifeless next to the side of the well.

"Hooray!" shouted Spes. "You saved her."

Saved her, he thought. The words screamed through his brain. He was overcome by an indescribable horror for within that gold box was a the most perfect heart-shaped ruby he had ever seen. It was large and beautiful, perfectly cut and polished and set in a delicate band of gold. It shined as bright as the princess's smile, and its color was as deep as his love for her. He knew without a doubt that it was the heart that would have saved her. Coniglio could not keep from sobbing.

Spes didn't understand. "What's wrong? You saved her. Why are you crying?" she asked, stepping close to Coniglio. She held Optare tightly in one arm, and reached to pat Coniglio with the other.

"Save her? No, I didn't save her. In fact, I just lost the only chance of saving her," he snapped at Spes.

"She's right here," Spes held Optare up for him to see.

"Not your doll. The princess," he cried, weeping into his hands.

"The princess needs water?" Spes was trying to understand.

"No. She needs a new heart, a perfect heart. Hers is frail and will fail her if she doesn't get a new one. I had the perfect heart in my vest pocket. It was the most beautiful thing I had ever seen. It would have saved her, but I lost it in the well while trying to save your doll." Coniglio continued to weep.

"You sound like you really love the princess," Spes said. She sat herself next to Coniglio and watched him cry.

"More than anything in this world," Coniglio responded. "But I have failed her."

"She needs a new heart?" Spes softly interrupted again.

"Yes, yes, a new heart," repeated Coniglio. Spes could tell that Coniglio was tiring of her continuous questions. She moved closer to Coniglio so he would know that he was not alone. There, holding Optare, she sat silently and listened as Coniglio cried. Her grandmother had told her once that sometimes the best thing that you can do when someone is very sad is sit quietly and listen to what their hearts say as they cry. So she did.

When Coniglio was calmer, Spes spoke softly to him, "I can help you?"

"That is a kind thought, little one," Coniglio replied. He was attempting to pull himself together. "I am afraid, though, that this is a problem much too big for a little girl like you to understand."

"But I can," Spes insisted. "You see, I have the perfect heart for you to give to the princess." Spes's excitement began to build. "It's at my home. It's not far. Come with me."

Weak and hopeless as Coniglio felt, he knew that he could

not allow a small child to go back into the woods alone. He would take the little girl to her home, collect her belongings and take her back with him. He knew that his mother and grandparents would welcome the young girl into their hearts. It was the right thing to do, the only thing to do.

Coniglio placed Spes on the horse and walked her through the woods to her small home. "Run and gather what you need. I will take you with me and you can meet my family. You will like them and I am sure they will love you. Hurry," Coniglio said. He lifted Spes off his horse.

Spes returned in a few moments. She had very little with her. In her hands she held her doll Optare, a small piece of cheese wrapped in a torn cloth (it was the last her grand-mother had made before she died), a worn out, pillow-look-ing thing, and the end of a rope. On the other end was a very old cow.

"I don't think that we can take your cow with us. She is very old and will slow us down," explained Coniglio.

"Oh, but we must. Betz might die without me. She needs me," Spes's wide blue eyes pleaded with Coniglio to under-stand. Coniglio knew the pain of loss and could bear no more. They would simply have to bring the cow.

Spes rode on Coniglio's horse, while Coniglio and Betz walked along beside them. "Here is the heart you need to give to the princess," Spes said as she lifted up the sagging bundle of worn pink velveteen.

Coniglio walked silently, lost in his hopeless thoughts. He did not have the heart to tell Spes that her pillow simply would not do. He changed the subject. "Speranza is an unusual name. What does it mean?"

"Hope," Spes replied with a smile.

"Hope. Hope does me no good now, my little one. For me, hope is gone." Coniglio thought wistfully of his childhood. How easy and carefree those years had been for him. He remembered reading in the garden, planting with his father, and believing in great possibilities. Gone from him now was the luxury of hope.

"But how can hope be gone, if I am here?" asked Spes. Her innocence was disarming.

"You are but a child. You cannot understand the complications of life. Hold on to your doll and your pillow, and trouble me no more with your childish questions," Coniglio said. He was not usually short or abrupt, but this was not a usual time. They walked quietly for a time.

"What is your name?" asked Spes interrupting the silence.

"My name is Coniglio," he answered, feeling a bit guilty for his sharpness earlier.

"What does it mean?" Spes continued.

"It means rabbit," Coniglio answered, wincing. There was nothing about his life that did not remind him of how he had failed the princess.

"I looooove rabbits," said Spes enthusiastically.

"You love them, eh?" smiled Coniglio. "Why?"

"Because they are soft and gentle and courageous," she answered, beaming.

"Courageous? Why would you think rabbits are courageous?" Coniglio asked, beginning to laugh. As impossible as it seemed, Spes's innocent and hopeful spirit were lifting his heavy heart.

"Because you are a rabbit and you risked your life to save Optare. That is the bravest thing anyone has ever done for her." Spes hugged her doll tightly and rocked her tiny body from side to side. "Here, take this," Spes said, handing him the worn pink bundle. "It is my precious heart, and now it belongs to you. My grandmother Agninas hand-stitched it for my mother out of a beautiful pink velveteen bag they found by the river. Mother said it was the greatest gift she had ever received, and just before she went to heaven, she gave it to me."

"And what of your father? What happened to him?" asked Coniglio.

"He died before I was born. Mother said he was wonder-fully handsome. I bet he looked like you," she said, blush-ing. "This heart is filled with treasure, you know. All my treasure is inside, and it will make up for the treasure you lost," Spes explained.

Coniglio smiled ruefully as he stuffed the pillow inside his vest. *It cannot make up for the treasure I lost*, Coniglio thought. He didn't want Spes to imagine that he did not appreciate her kind offer. *How could she understand, she was just a child?* He sadly mused. *She has never seen real treasure. Besides, what could a child know of hearts, and how to heal them when they are broken?*

hose in attendance who were brave enough to look upon the princess's face saw the light in her eyes beginning to dim."

Twelve

Offering of Hearts

It was the day before the princess's twenty-first birthday, the official day of the contest. And though the king was worried about the princess; the princess was worried sick about Coniglio. For days she had been wondering where he was and if he was all right. The contest was about to begin and Coniglio was still nowhere to be found. It wasn't like him, but she knew that losing his father, his home, and the Empress heart box (a month ago he had told her about it in his excitement), must have caused him great distress and sadness. She wanted to speak to him, see his face, and comfort him, but where was he?

The trumpets sounded and the princess was carried into the large, open marble meeting hall. Her chair was placed next to her father's throne. Through the sea of faces, her eyes searched in vain for Coniglio.

Those in attendance who were brave enough to look upon the princess's face saw the light in her eyes beginning to dim. She looked more fragile and pale than normal. Today she was dressed in a lovely flowing gown. It was simple and elegant, and matched the nature of the princess.

The people of the kingdom did not really know the princess, other than seeing her through the garden gates. She had never been well enough to travel or make speeches. The large marble hall was filled with a strange morbid curiosity.

Did the old man tell the truth so long ago? Would she die tomorrow unless offered the perfect heart?

The trumpets sounded again and all stood except the princess, for she had grown too weak to stand on her own. The king entered the great hall. As he walked toward his throne, his eyes met the eyes of the princess. *Oh, how he loved her*, he thought sadly, turning toward his people as he reached his throne.

"This is an important day for our kingdom," the king stated weakly, his voice breaking with his heart. He knew he would not be able to deliver the speech he had prepared. His heart was aching, and nothing seemed important in all of these charades. "Let the contestants make their offerings," the king continued, sitting down.

The first to present his heart was the warrior prince. The greatest craftsman from his country had worked tirelessly for weeks crafting the magnificent heart-adorned sword that the young prince now offered. It was fashioned from the finest steel and had been shaped and sharpened into a magnificent weapon. At the shank between the handle and the birth of the blade was an intricately carved heart sitting on a crest of gold overlay. In the center of the heart was an ornate letter "C" representing Cortellus, the country that the princess loved so deeply.

The prince stepped forward proudly and challenged the greatest warriors of Cortellus to fight him. The king selected five of his finest swordsmen and upon the prince's insistence, ordered them to charge the prince simultaneously. There were gasps of terror from the citizens in the crowd as they watched the soldiers' blades meet with savage power. The women turned their heads as the prince one by one left the fine swordsmen wounded and bleeding on the floor. The king's guards helped the wounded men out of the throne room.

Upon his victory he turned to the king and confidently stated, "A princess needs the heart of a warrior to defend and protect her. She needs to know that her lands will be protected from invasion and that her subjects will without fail honor and praise her name. She needs the courage that a great warrior can give to her. She needs the strength and wisdom that come with the scars of war, and the thrill of victory. The princess is frail and many will believe that she can easily be taken advantage of. She needs a heart of steel to fortify her, to alter what has up to this time been perceived as weakness, and turn herself and her kingdom over to strength. I offer my sword, my will, my courage, and with it, the perfect heart for a princess so fair and frail."

With that, the prince turned and walked proudly back to stand in line with the other contestants.

The second contestant was the jeweler. He had spent the last weeks perfecting the casting for the gold setting. He had cut and polished each diamond with the meticulous care he was known for. The finished product was breathtaking. He could not wait to present his masterpiece to the princess, for he was sure that he was the one who had created the perfect heart for a queen.

The jeweler stepped close to the steps of the throne room and carried in his hands a small dark mahogany box trimmed with gold edging. He had crafted tiny gold nails and a gold clasp, making the case exquisite enough to match the masterpiece inside.

He spoke clearly and chose his words carefully. "My great king and dear princess, I have brought to you this perfect heart of magnificent quality because after all, a queen must first and foremost be looked upon as a woman of great quality. This fine box is filled with a heart that is most wonderful. It contains a three-carat, heart-shaped diamond surrounded by twenty-one flawless princess-cut diamonds."

The jeweler carefully opened the box with the elegance and finesse one would use to open the most magnificent bottle of fine wine. The diamonds instantly caught the light and reflected it throughout the room. It was as though there were millions of tiny diamonds bouncing from one place to another, like fairies dancing a dance of delight. Sighs and gasps of awe filled the hall. This was indeed one of the most beautiful sights the king or any of his subjects had ever seen.

"I chose this symbol for the princess because a princess needs to be exquisitely adorned at all times," the jeweler said with complete conviction. "A princess's heart should be as flawless and perfect as my gift. Also, diamonds are the hardest substance known to man, and likewise, it will be impossible for the princess's heart to ever be broken. Diamonds reflect the light as a princess's heart should reflect the light in her people's eyes. A great princess must stand out from everyone. This unique diamond heart necklace will speak of her value and worth so that no one in the kingdom can ever deny her birthright as queen. She will sparkle in the sunlight and all those who catch sight of her great adornment with be humbled by its beauty." All the people were in awe of the perfection of the jeweler's offering.

Meanwhile, the tall, fair-skinned man stood quietly in line, caressing a small object hidden in his robes. He had guarded until the last moment before he was to present it.

"I offer this gift for two reasons," he said, "for it consists of two very different things that would lose meaning without each other. Here, great King, is a crystal heart flacon filled with the most precious fragrance in the world. I have named the perfume 'Royalty.' It will belong only to the princess. As she wears her sweet fragrance, all who come into her presence will be reverent and respectful. The scent of fine perfume calls forth an emotional reaction. It is a sign of elegance, wealth, and royalty, and it lingers long after the person wearing it is gone. A queen needs to linger in the minds of her subjects."

The man continued, "The crystal bottle holding the fragrance symbolizes beauty and protection. Without its container, the perfume is vulnerable to the elements. A princess should be blessed with both beauty and protection. Crystal is created when raging fire melts sand into glass. This crystal bottle is a symbol of how hearts should melt for their queen." He paused for emphasis.

"Clearly, the two elements of my gift symbolize the perfect heart for a queen," the man said. He stepped back, cupping the marvelous offering in his hands.

The next to step forward was the artist. The people snickered as they observed his bright multi-colored clothing trimmed in various beads and tassels. He held himself with a solemn passion that soon quieted the laughter. He was carrying a large square object covered with muslin and an easel. As he approached the steps of the throne, he carefully unfolded the easel that he had balanced under his arm. Once convinced that it was steady, he gently sat the large flat square object on the easel, and gracefully unveiled the masterpiece beneath.

There was a great, unified gasp throughout the palace

throne room. The painting was gorgeous. It captured the light like a placid lake captures the sun and turns it into diamonds flickering on the water. It was in the shape of a classical heart but the texture and colors caused the painting to feel alive with motion. This was surely a masterpiece, a treasure unlike the rest.

"A future queen's responsibility to her subjects extends far beyond the practices of everyday life," the artist said. "These things merely sustain basic existence, but art liberates people on a much higher level. It teaches the unlimited possibilities that creativity brings to our lives. It is the gift on which all great societies will be judged long after their everyday efforts have passed away. Great art lives on for centuries. I have painted the perfect heart for a queen, for this is a heart driven by the passion of expression that will inspire the subjects of our kingdom, and of many kingdoms, for generations to come."

With that, the artist bowed and backed away, carefully carrying the painting and the easel with him.

As the banker neared the king, he motioned for his servants to pull a large covered figure toward the king. It was obviously extremely heavy because it took thirty men pulling with all of their might to force the great form across the granite, inlaid floor of the palace. The banker stood proudly as the men struggled. Once in place, he dismissed his servants with a wave, and reached for the cords that held the canvas covering the statue.

The banker pulled the cords, allowing the canvas to drop gently to the floor around the statue. The banker's cheeks were flushed with confidence. He was sure that his offering was by far the most expensive and beautiful. There were whispers in the crowd, for the excitement around the sheer magnificence of the statue could not be contained. Weeks before, after drawing one of the seven numbers, the banker had taken a large wagon of gold to the foundry. There he had a life-sized statue of the princess cast. Her hands were sculpted to gently cup a magnificent heart in front of her chest. Truly, the statue was exquisite. It captured the beauty and sensitivity of the princess.

The banker cleared his throat. "A queen needs a heart of gold, a heart that is symbolic of her value to the kingdom. A queen should be recognized as a great treasure and held in the highest of esteem. She should be on display as a reminder of her status and perfection. Gold is considered the most valuable substance. It is respected in all lands near and far. When this statue is looked upon, it will remind all who view it that their queen has worth beyond compare. It will stand as a legacy of royalty for generations to come. Every great queen should have a heart of gold."

The audience broke out in cheers. The statue was indeed a great and wonderful offering.

The sixth man waited until the room was quiet again. His dark hair was pulled back and his dark eyes were focused. He glided effortlessly toward the steps beneath the king. It was as if his feet did not touch the floor as he walked. Everyone was curious about this man.

He bowed to the king, then spoke, "I bring the magic of illusion to the princess, for everyone loves a heart filled with magic." There was a flash of light, and suddenly out of nowhere appeared a rabbit in the man's arms. "Would it please the princess to have the heart of a rabbit?"

The princess had sadness in her eyes. "Yes, it would," she answered as her thoughts filled with Coniglio and his rabbit heart.

The man spun and twirled with the grace of a dancer, the strength of a warrior, and the cunning of a fox. As he spun, he pulled colored cloth from thin air, made flowers appear, juggled silver balls of light in the air, and finally, in the grandest move of all, he pulled a dark drape, revealing a lion. The spectators gasped in fear as the lion roared. "Or would it please the princess to have the heart of a lion?" A twist of his cape, and the lion was gone again.

Applause broke out throughout the large hall. No one had ever seen such a wonderful display.

"The princess needs a heart filled with magic, for hers is frail and weak. I bring to you, my princess, whatever heart you desire. A heart filled with magic is a heart that believes in possibility, opportunity, and miracles. I bring to you the perfect magic heart." Once again there was applause, for the illusionist had stirred great excitement in the hearts of the people of Cortellus.

The princess nodded with deep appreciation as her eyes searched for the face her heart longed to see. *Where is he?* she wondered. She could feel her heart weakening. Time was closing in on her.

earts are not perfect. As we go through life, we will lose people we love. At other times we will find that people disappoint us, hurt us and make us terribly sad. That is why my grandmother made my heart of cloth, so it would not easily be broken, and on those occasions that it is torn apart, love could easily stitch it back together."

Thirteen

The Last Contestant

Spes and Coniglio were standing at the edge of the hall. They had arrived just in time to watch the contestants one by one. Spes was clapping, laughing and giggling, while Coniglio stood silently, watching. He was amazed by all of the hearts brought to the princess, and he felt certain that one of them, because of their perfection and magnificence, would save the woman he loved.

Coniglio was glad that Alba had so many fine hearts to choose from, but his own heart was breaking. Of course, if one of these men could save her, then that was all that really mattered. He could bear losing her to another as long as she was safe and well.

If only I could have brought the princess the perfect ruby, I might stand a chance against the rest, he thought. But the ruby was gone, and all that was left was a worn-out pillow and his humiliation.

A silence fell over the room. Everyone was waiting for the seventh contestant.

"Number seven? Where is the seventh contestant?" one of the king's aides called.

Spes tugged at Coniglio's jacket. Her big blue eyes were filled with courage. "Go. Give her your heart," she encouraged. "You are the last one. It is your turn. You must give it to her now."

Coniglio's heart was breaking. He didn't want to hurt Spes's feelings. He knew that she loved the small worn heart and believed it to be precious, but his pride kept insisting that he not make a fool of himself. How could he present an old velveteen pillow to his princess? How could he place it next to diamonds and gold? How could he compete with the courage behind the sword of a great warrior, or the awesome magic of the illusionist? His princess deserved magic. In fact, she deserved all of the hearts offered to her. If only he had his Empress box, or that beautiful ruby ring.

Coniglio did not doubt that when Spes's grandmother had sewn the soft cloth heart for her daughter that the velveteen was the most beautiful pink. But even new, velveteen was considered a poor man's fabric, certainly not held with the same regard of brocades and fine furs. And now, the pink had been loved off, leaving the small pillow threadbare in places. He was sure that at one time the lace had been white and carefully sewn, but the lace was now dingy and the stitching that had once held the pillows shape was loosening. It was obvious that the pillow had been stitched together again and again.

Spes was becoming impatient. "Go Coniglio! Go," she insisted. "Everyone is waiting on you. Give her your heart."

Coniglio knelt down to Spes's level so that his eyes could meet hers. "Spes," he whispered carefully, "I cannot present this heart to the princess. For one thing, it is not really mine; it is yours."

"No it isn't, not anymore. I gave it to you. That is what our hearts are for, to be given to others," Spes said as the light danced in her eyes. "Remember, I told you, my grandmother Agninas made it for my mother Dolce, and she gave it to me. I gave it to you, and it is yours. Now go and give it to the princess, for each time it is given it becomes more wonderful."

"But the princess is very frail," Coniglio argued. "Her heart is failing her. She needs a perfect heart in order for her to survive. I know that you think that the heart in my vest is wonderful, but that is because you have grown to love it. Look at it, Spes." Coniglio held the ragged pillow in front of her. "Can't you see that it is worn and torn, and looks terribly tired?"

"But Grandmother told me that is what makes a heart more beautiful. Hearts are not perfect. As we go through life, we will lose people we love. At other times we will find that people disappoint us, hurt us and make us terribly sad. That is why my grandmother made my heart of cloth, so it would not easily be broken, and on those occasions that it is torn apart, love could easily stitch it back together."

"I don't know what to think anymore." Coniglio sighed. All he knew was that if he refused Spes's request, her heart would be broken. Coniglio closed his eyes, and remembered the day he met the princess. He remembered what she had told him when he was embarrassed and humiliated.

I think that it takes the greatest strength to be gentle. I think it takes greatest courage to be willing to sacrifice your heart for the heart of another. To me, my dear rabbit, your parents have done you a great service. Besides, I see you as one of the strongest, keenest, bravest people that I have ever met.

If he didn't risk the laughter and humiliation of this act,

Spes's heart would surely be broken. He knew that it was the right thing to do for her sake, and he trusted that though others would not understand his reasons, the princess would trust that they had merit, for she had always trusted his heart.

"Number seven? Step forward now or loose your standing as a contestant," the king's aide insisted.

"Princess Alba." Coniglio spoke her name clearly as he stepped from the crowd of people. The princess's heart felt alive for the first time that day. Coniglio bowed in her presence as he had done hundreds of times before. "Sire," he turned toward the king and bowed again with great respect. "I am the man who drew the number seven. I bring but a humble gift. It looks much different from the rest," he said as he raised the pillow carefully in his hands, his body filled with courage. Laughter spread throughout the room. No one could imagine anyone offering such a pitiful gift to the princess.

The king's face showed the shock he felt. He could not hide his disappointment.

Coniglio stood in silence. He had so much to give, but it was of no use now. He had stepped out in faith, doing what was necessary in order to protect the innocent heart of a child. The laughter grew louder. No one but the princess could possibly understand his reasons, and no one but the princess knew what to do next.

He understood their ...

 he understood their motivations, and had words for each of them. She was grateful for the hours of reading that she had shared with Coniglio, for it was through the wisdom in those books that she had learned what was necessary to save the heart of a great queen."

Fourteen

A Warrior's Heart

The princess felt all eyes on her, awaiting her reaction, curious about what choice she would make. Her subjects watched her struggle to stand. The king immediately motioned for the princess's guards to come to her aid, but as they neared, she respectfully stopped them with a wave of her hand. She looked into the faces of the seven contestants, and considered their diverse and marvelous offerings. A new light in her eyes was shining so brightly that it was obvious she was deeply moved by what had been offered to her. She felt a strange unusual strength fill her body, and she held herself with a new grace and poise.

She scanned the room and carefully looked into the eyes of her people. She could see the worry and concern that was heavy on their hearts. They knew, as did she, that the choice she made this day would either serve as her new beginning or her end.

Once again, she turned her eyes toward the seven men that had come to offer their hearts. She was moved by their generosity, even though she knew that most of them had only pretended to consider her as they created their hearts of perfection.

She understood their motivations, and had words for each of them. She was grateful for the hours of reading that she had shared with Coniglio, for it was through the wisdom in those books that she had learned what was necessary to save the heart of a great queen.

The princess stepped toward the strong warrior. She could see that underneath his apparent fortitude lived a child driven to protect himself from the pain of disappointment. She knew he wanted to be able to control what happened in the world so that he might control what could happen to him.

"Thank you, great prince," she said. "You are tall and strong, both in body and in will. All you believe, you carry with pride and power. You have intended to do me a great service by taking the burden of ruling a great kingdom from me, and placing it on your back. Indeed you are a capable, strong, and willful warrior and your offering pleases me greatly."

The prince held his body strong, for his heart was bursting with pride. "Thank you, princess. I vow to serve you with my best," he stated boldly, bowing his head as a soldier might salute a respected officer.

"I trust your heart completely, but I cannot select the heart that you have offered. You see, you believe that your way is not only the right way, but the only way. You are willing to sacrifice your life, and the lives of others, in order to change that which you decide is not aligned with what you believe.

"Thank you for your offering, but a great queen needs a heart filled with understanding and a thirst for knowledge of those things that appear different. The heart you offer would cut away such understanding, leaving me lifeless on my throne.

The princess moved closer to the prince. "You have been

called to be mighty, but your beliefs serve as a prison that refuses to set the real strength inside of you free." She bowed before him in deep respect. "Your need to be right cripples your ability to understand."

Everything in the prince wanted to fight. She is wrong, he thought to himself, and yet his very thoughts were proving that she was wise in her assessment. "I don't understand," the prince began to argue. "I would die for what I believe to be best for you and this kingdom."

"Yes, I know," said the princess softly as she rose from her bow. "The more important question is, would you be willing to die so that everyone might have the right to their own beliefs, even if you disagreed with them and deemed them wrong?"

"No, I could not," the prince replied quickly. "I could never protect what I believed to be weak, immoral or wrong."

"I understand," the princess said, again nodding gracefully. She turned and walked toward the jeweler.

*Y*ou say that diamonds are unbreakable, something I hope never to be. Breaking is a part of learning to love fully. We are reminded of this as the dawn lovingly breaks for us over and over again; not sadly, but with great joy, for with each break of day, we begin anew. As we face the inevitable breaks of life, may we choose not to be broken down, but instead, broken open like a newborn eagle, open to hope, open to vision, open to soaring once again."

Fifteen

Unbreakable Stones

The princess stepped close to the jeweler. "It is apparent that you are a great master in your field, and that you have spent weeks creating this brilliant piece. I salute you, for your creation has left me breathless."

"Thank you," the jeweler said, wiping the beads of sweat from his brow.

She continued, "There is no doubt that this necklace is made of the finest stones. And your intention of insuring that a queen is looked upon as a woman of quality is commendable. However, I would rather be compared to the box in which your masterpiece was kept, for I believe that a great queen is not defined by what she wears on the outside but what she lives on the inside." The princess smiled, though she could see that the jeweler was distressed.

"What you have created here is flawless. I can see why you would, with great confidence, bring this perfect heart to an ailing princess. However, real hearts are not flawless. Each of us has survived times when our hearts were injured and wounded. Many of us have been left with scars that run deep and wide from experiences in our pasts. If diamonds are to symbolize our hearts—the heart of a queen or the heart of a peasant struggling to feed his family—let the diamonds have many flaws, but set them in gold bands of forgiveness. It is those times when we ask forgiveness that are golden."

The princess continued, "We are all frightened, frightened of feeling the intense pain of rejection and humiliation, but in protecting ourselves from the pain, we lose much of what makes us unique and wonderful."

The jeweler's eyes began to moisten. He was remembering the pain he had fought so hard to escape.

"You have been hurt, my dear jeweler, as have I. Growing up I was unable to play, run and dance with other children. Because I was different, they made fun of what they did not understand. My heart is not perfect; I have the courage to admit that with my subjects. I do not desire perfection, for perfection does not require love."

The princess spoke with great conviction, "You say that a great queen should be greatly adorned. On this point I must agree with you, although my choice of adornment is different from that which you have offered. I choose to be adorned like our mighty Empress trees, which have grown to become the symbol of Cortellus. That which I inspire to bloom will adorn me, just as the radiant violet blossoms adorn the trees. I will dedicate my life to inspiring my subjects to bloom in knowledge, understanding, and compassion. Their kind acts toward one another will be the jewels in my crown.

You say that diamonds are unbreakable, something I hope never to be. Breaking is a part of learning to love fully. We are reminded of this as the dawn lovingly breaks for us over and over again; not sadly, but with great joy, for with each break of day, we begin anew. As we face the inevitable breaks of life, may we choose not to be broken down, but instead, broken open like a newborn eagle, open to hope, open to vision, open to soaring once again."

The jeweler began to weep. "Thank you, princess, for in your decision to not choose my perfect heart of diamonds, you have chosen my flawed heart of feelings."

Princess Alba smiled. "And now I must make a request."

"Anything," said the jeweler.

"I want you to design simple yet elegant rings consisting of a simple band with a small heart attached. In the heart, you shall place a small flawed stone. The design will be known as the 'Heart of Cortellus.' These rings will remind each of us that although flawed, we are beautiful and forgiving. Let the rings be sold for the cost of the stones, the gold, and the time it takes to craft them. I will support the craftsmen you select for this project as long as they are men and women who come from very poor families. Are you willing to serve your kingdom in this way?"

"Without question," the jeweler responded. His tears of pain were now tears of joy. This was a great opportunity to help those who were suffering like he had. The princess's words sparkled in his heart brighter than any diamond.

"You have been called," said the princess, "and you have chosen to set yourself and in the process others free from the illusion of perfection. For your courage, I will treasure your perfect but flawed heart always."

For the first time in the jeweler's life, he felt worthy, and the citizens were inspired and touched again by the grace of the princess.

*Y*ou were correct
when you said that
fragrance has for
centuries been recognized as one of the finest
offerings one person can give to another."

Sixteen

A Lingering Legacy

The fair-skinned man stood nervously. The princess approached him and smiled. "You gift is comprised of two very different gifts that compliment each other. Their symbols and your insight have blessed me and have deeply touched my heart. You called my special fragrance 'Royalty' because it is fit for a queen. I have a request for you, my fine gentleman. Can you teach my subjects to collect and crush the petals and add the fine oils to duplicate this rare and wonderful fragrance?"

"Yes, my princess, but why?" asked the man.

"Because I love the gift so much that I want to share it with all of my subjects. I only ask for one small change," Princess Alba replied.

"What is that?" asked the perfumer, struck by the princess's ability to make everyone feel special in her presence.

"My request is that you change the 'R' in Royalty to an 'L' for Loyalty. The letter 'R' is symbolic of words like right, rigidity and revenge. These are words that set people apart from one another. The letter 'L' is symbolic of words like love, laughter, and light. These are all words of inclusiveness. My request is that you teach my people how to share and be loyal to one another. You were correct when you said that fragrance has for centuries been recognized as one of the finest offerings one person can give to another. The scent of perfume does call forth an emotional reaction; I want that reaction to be one of unity. I would like for this magnificent fragrance to become another of our kingdom's trademarks, like our Empress trees. And I want our commitment to one another to linger long after we physically leave the earth. The thought of a queen may not need to linger in the minds of her subjects, but the loyalty we have for one another should. For if loyalty becomes our trademark, if care and concern become those things that linger in our hearts, then Cortellus will become as the beautiful crystal flacon that you offered. It will be a place of beauty and protection that can keep all who live here sheltered from the cruelty of others. As raging fires melt sand into glass, let our love, laughter, and light melt the anger, judgment and cruelty in our hearts. Will you guide and teach our people to create loyalty and love?"

The perfumer was shocked. Never had he felt such an awesome pounding in his chest. He had longed for a purpose, a legacy to leave behind him, and magically the princess had made it a reality. To her, his desire had been clear as crystal. "Thank you, my future queen," he said. "It will be my great honor to serve in such an important capacity." He knelt in loyalty.

"You have been called to linger in the hearts of Cortellus and to leave the legacy of loyalty. Thank you. Your commitment to me and my people fills my heart like your beautiful perfume fills the crystal flacon."

The people of the kingdom were once again touched by the wisdom of their princess.

ou have been called to bring life to expression, and I thank you for choosing to express your passion and talent in this beautiful way," the princess said. She reached for the artist's hand and gently kissed it. "It is hands like this that create beauty for the world to share."

Seventeen

The Art of Heart

The short, squatty man was nervously playing with his mustache as the princess approached him. His anxiety betrayed his serious nature. He stepped backwards toward the easel and almost knocked the beautiful painting to the floor.

"Your painting is a wonderful collection of color and texture," the princess said as she stepped close to the canvas. "I love the way it captures the light." She reached out to gently feel the texture of the painting. "It is obvious to all that this is a true masterpiece, a treasure unlike the rest."

The artist took his first breath in several moments. He was delighted that the princess understood the great and undeniable value of art. "Thank you, my princess; your response delights me." His bright smile barely showed under his heavy mustache.

The princess continued, "Although I agree with you completely that a queen's responsibility to her subjects extends far beyond the practices of everyday life, I must add to your assessment. I believe that similar to creating a great painting, a great queen must be willing to build her kingdom one step at a time."

Everyone listened carefully, not wanting to miss the profound wisdom of their young princess.

"First, the wooden frame must be constructed," she said. "It must be strong and able to hold the canvas in place for many years to come. The frame of any society is the basic needs, the food, water, and shelter that people must have in order to have the physical strength to care about anything else. Next, the canvas must be cut and fit to its frame. This act is called stretching. It is critical for a great queen and her subjects to understand the need to stretch themselves to become more, give more, and do more.

"People are very similar to art," she continued. "It is only in taking care of the mundane that we find ourselves safe enough to begin the expression process. A sense of safety gives wings to the expression that lives in our hearts. I am committed to both but I need your help in order to succeed."

"Of course, my princess," the artist said. "What can I do?"

"I would like for you to open a school of painting, sculpture, and design. I would like for it to be connected with a museum that I plan to commission and leave to the subjects of Cortellus and to the travelers that come to partake of the wonders of the museum."

"That would be a great honor, my queen." The artist was wild with enthusiasm. For many years he had attempted to convince those in power to help support the arts but they had not understood the benefits that great art brings to the lives of all who partake of it.

"You have been called to bring life to expression, and I thank you for choosing to express your passion and talent in this beautiful way," the princess said. She reached for the artist's hand and gently kissed it. "It is hands like this that create beauty for the world to share."

The people were ecstatic. They knew without doubt that the princess would be an extraordinary ruler.

he gold that I have witnessed thus far today came from no earthen mine."

Eighteen

Hearts of Gold

The princess approached the banker more slowly than the rest. She was concerned that her words would have little meaning to the mind of a mathematical man. She noticed, though, that his face, which used to look lifeless, was radiant.

Yesterday, none of this made any sense to him. Even this morning, he could barely understand what he knew he had to say. "Before you begin, my dear queen," he said, "I know that this great statue will not be selected as your perfect heart. The gold that I have witnessed thus far today came from no earthen mine. You do not need this statue, for you are not driven by your own recognition and power. Your heart, weak as it is, is already golden. You need no tall statue of status or perfection, for you are a living and breathing example of how tall a human being can stand on the earth.

"Until today, I thought that gold was the currency of the most high, but watching you walk in such grace and wisdom today, I understand that there is a much greater currency than gold could ever be—the currency of love. Your heart already shines as a beacon to others. You have no need of this massive gold statue. It cannot serve you in any way." The banker bowed his head in reverence.

"Oh but it can," reassured the princess. "I need you to melt it down and shape it back into coins. Then, take this currency that is so respected by the world and use it to fund the hospital that our kingdom so desperately needs." The princess paused and smiled at her future subjects.

She continued, "I have another request, knowing that you are a genius with finances. Make all of the money you can and teach others to do the same. Then, give a good portion of your money to benefit the lives of those who do not share your gift.

"You will forever be known as the man with the golden heart who taught and inspired others to succeed and to give of their abundance. A queen does not need a heart of gold as badly as she needs her people to possess golden hearts. Your heart will truly shine forever, and a small portion of this statue will be used to make my crown so that forever you will know that your generosity crowns me with glory, not simply with gold."

The banker's heart was abundant. Never had he felt so rich. With tears of gratitude he accepted the princess's offer.

"What could she say that would give value to the nothingness he had in his heart."

Nineteen

Making Something Out of Nothing

he illusionist wished that he could make himself disappear. He had watched the princess make something valuable of each offering, but he did not know how she could make something valuable out of nothing. An illusion is simply that, an illusion. What could she say that would give value to the nothingness he had in his heart?

The princess smiled as she approached the man. "My dear illusionist," she said, "are you wondering about the true value of what you have brought to me?"

"Why yes! How did you know?" asked the illusionist, amazed.

"Magic," the princess softly teased. The illusionist smiled with her, for he could see that the princess's heart was sincere. "What you have offered me has immense value. In fact, none of the hearts offered could exist without your gift."

The illusionist was confused, as were many of the people watching.

The princess continued, "You have brought to me the gift of imagination. Illusion is nothing more than an opportunity to dream the seemingly impossible. If each of my fine contestants had not dreamed and seen a possibility before it was a reality, none of them would be here today. The warrior saw the possibility of leading a great kingdom. The jeweler saw the possibility of creating a necklace of perfect stones. The perfumer believed he could create a unique and royal fragrance before he went to pick the petals and combine them with oils. The artist pictured his original work before it was brought to life on the canvas. The banker saw in his mind a great sculpture of gold before the gold was melted and formed. And yet, none of them imagined how their gifts would be transformed, as you also could never imagine how your gift has allowed a princess to see more clearly than ever before. I now understand how a queen can be strengthened by many hearts, all perfect in different ways." The princess had never felt so strong, alive, happy, and fulfilled.

She continued, "I have a great request, my dear illusionist. I beg you to stay and make Cortellus your home. Please teach my kingdom the magic of great dreams. Inspire them and teach them to look for what their fear tells them is impossible. It is only when our dreams become as big as we imagine that we fulfill our greatest potential and the purpose for which we were born."

The illusionist was mesmerized. How had she seen so clearly what was in his heart? He did have a dream bigger than the dream that his father had chosen for him. His father could not imagine anything else, so he had created illusions for others because the life he longed to live seemed impossible. "How can I serve you, Princess? I am afraid that I do not know where to begin," confessed the illusionist.

Princess Alba smiled with excitement. "If you could create the greatest dream in your heart, what would it be?"

"A circus," the illusionist said, beaming, "a circus filled with animals, magic, and laugher. I want to create a circus that reminds all who come to see it of the wonders and miracles of life. And from that circus I would create a wonderful zoo, a world of animals that would inspire the curiosity and dreams of children."

"A circus it is," nodded the princess. "I would like for you to begin work on it tomorrow."

The people cheered with glee and the children danced. No one in Cortellus ever imagined that they would have something as fine as a circus or a zoo full of wonderful animals. This was almost too good to be true.

He had never seen her so radiant or strong, the color of her eyes so deep. Each word she had spoken confirmed that she was all her name spoke her to be. She was the sun, rising out of darkness, bringing warmth and light to all she touched."

Twenty

A Heart That's Full

The princess turned toward Coniglio. He had never seen her so radiant or strong, the color of her eyes so deep. Each word she had spoken confirmed that she was all her name spoke her to be. She was the sun, rising out of darkness, bringing warmth and light to all she touched. He was speechless.

Princess Alba approached him. "You were the only contestant that did not explain the meaning of the heart you offered. I need to hear your explanation before I can respond," she said. Her face was familiar; her eyes were safe; her smile was tender. Looking at her gave Coniglio the courage to speak.

"I offer this simple heart to you because it has been well-loved by many." He glanced back at Spes, whose eyes were filled with delight. He turned back to the princess. "You can see love's wear on this pillow just as you can see love in the eyes of those who choose it." Coniglio lifted up the pillow to show its obvious wear. "When something is loved well for a long, long time, it may look as though it is aged and worn, but in truth it becomes more wonderful with each passing year. Some could look at this pillow and think that it is simply worn out, but ask any child who has ever loved their pillow, or blanket, or favorite toy, and they will tell you how very loved and real they are. A princess needs a heart that has been loved well, but more than that, a princess needs a heart that is real."

The king thought of Caritas. With each passing year she had become more beautiful. He remembered the thinning skin on her hands, the tiny age spots that appeared from nowhere, and the silver that took over her dark silken hair. He remembered looking at her lying on her pillow the day she said goodbye, and thinking she was more beautiful than all the days before. Coniglio was right. When something or someone is loved for a long time, they are more wonderful than the finest jewels and riches one can own.

Coniglio motioned to Spes, who rushed to his side. "This is my friend Speranza. Those who know her call her Spes. Her name means hope, and though she is small, she has the heart of a lion." Spes smiled and playfully bowed. "Spes gave this heart to me. Her grandmother stitched it and gave it as a birthday gift to Spes's mother, Dolce. Spes's mother loved it well, and then gave it to Spes. Although this was all Spes had left of her family legacy, she sacrificed her precious heart for my benefit and the benefit of another."

Coniglio gently pulled on the opening of the pillow. He reached inside to expose Spes's treasure. He was beginning to understand. "This heart is a heart filled with magic, the magic of a child's imagination and faith. Within this heart you will find great treasures unlike others you have seen today." Coniglio poured the contents into his hand. There was a piece of string, a blue feather, a stone, a pressed flower, a pearl, and a small candle.

"Spes can you tell me why these treasures fill your heart?" Coniglio asked.

"They all mean something. They remind me of what my mother and grandmother taught me," answered Spes.

"What does the string mean?" asked Coniglio as he picked it up from the floor.

"It reminds me to focus on what is important. Grandmother used to tie this string to her finger to help her remember. She said that we must remember to make time for those things that are important because if we don't, the things that aren't can get in the way."

"What does the blue feather symbolize?" asked Coniglio, handing the feather to Spes.

"Mother found it one day while we were walking. She gave it to me and said, 'Let this feather remind you to never lose hope. Hope is as light as a feather, yet it can carry the weight of life's heaviest burdens. Hope gives wings to our dreams. Dreams were made to soar, but only we can give them flight." Spes stroked the feather and straightened it where its edges were ruffled.

"What about this stone?" Coniglio handed it to her.

Spes closed her eyes and rubbed it between her thumb and fingers. "My grandmother gave it to me. She found it in the river and told me that I should build my life on the stones of faith and integrity, for without either, life was less than it was meant to be."

"And this pressed flower?" continued Coniglio.

"Mother gave me the flower when she was dying. Daddy was waiting for her in heaven. I was crying. She picked the flower, and told me that all things must pass. It is the circle of life. Just as spring brings the flowers, fall steals the leaves. That is why it is important to take no season for granted, and to waste not a minute of today." Spes put the string, the feather, the rock and the pressed flower back inside the heart.

"What about this pearl?" Coniglio gently placed it in Spes's small hands.

"The pearl is special. It is from my mother's favorite necklace. She told me that pearls begin as problems for an oyster. They start as small pieces of sand that cause discomfort and irritation—like our problems. Mother said that whenever there is a problem, it is simply an opportunity to make pearls in our lives," Spes said. She opened her hand and looked hard at the pearl. "I know that mother would want me to, but I don't know how to make a pearl out of losing my grandmother. I am afraid of being all alone." In a flash, Spes's face changed from happy to very sad.

"Don't be afraid, Spes. I know how to help you make it a pearl," said Coniglio. He hugged her and reached for the last treasure from the pillow. "What about this small candle?"

"The candle is from my birthday cake," she replied. "My grandmother said that I should keep it to remind me what a gift life is meant to be. Life is no brief candle but a torch to be held up for all to witness the brightness of its light. We are born with a purpose, and it is up to us to find it, use it, and make the world a better place. She said that the candle should remind me that miracles are real, and that it is up to me to be one." Spes took the candle and the pearl and slipped them inside the heart where they belonged. She hugged the pillow tightly to her chest and handed it back to Coniglio.

Coniglio said, "This heart is also important, my princess, because it is a pillow. Real love does not break hearts; it is unable to, but real love can break the inevitable falls caused by life's disappointments. I cannot offer what others can, my princess, but like this pillow, I can give you my promise that my heart will always be there to break your fall. I cannot offer you a perfect heart, but I can offer you one full of love, wonder, wisdom, and miracles." With that, the princess took the pillow and held it to her heart. Tears filled her eyes, for the pleasure of the gift was too much for words.

"I choose this one," she said, ready for whatever consequences might accompany her choice. The room was completely still. A tear of great joy dropped from the cheek of the princess onto the heart she held tightly to her chest, and like magic, the heart became new again. The pink velveteen was new, bright, soft and shiny, the lace was lovely and white, the stitching perfect and careful. The princess, too, felt stronger than she had ever felt before.

Her heart, like the pillow, was new and old, strong and soft, wise and childlike, open to possibility but closed to prejudice and hatred. It was full of love and made to love. It was willing to break as the dawn breaks each day, while capable of breaking the fall of others in despair. It had wings to soar, and was filled with hope. It was filled with integrity and rock-solid reverence for herself and others. It was a heart that would always remember what was important, while never forgetting to appreciate the wonderful gift of life. It was a combination of all she had ever learned, and all she had ever been offered. Her heart was perfect, and it was Coniglio's love that kept it beating strong.

*hey showered her with
love and taught her how
to read."*

Twenty One

$\mathcal{L}$ife and its $\mathcal{P}$riceless $\mathcal{G}$ifts

oniglio and Princess Alba were married at dawn the next morning in a small ceremony. Coniglio and Princess Alba welcomed Spes into their new family. They showered her with love and taught her how to read.

As a wedding present, the king ordered that the most mature of the Empress trees be harvested to build a large library, filled with the hundreds of books that Conoscenzo had gathered over the years. The library was named the Library of Conoscenzo, a pleasing legacy for the loving scholar.

And a few years later, after looking upon the face of his daughter's firstborn son, the kind old king went back to his bed and passed away in his sleep. He was smiling when they found him. Coniglio and Queen Alba named their new son Anthony, after the man who began his life as Pomus. Anthony means priceless gift, and that is what Pomus became, for he spent the rest of his days offering the priceless gift of faith to everyone he met.

*N*ames and their *M*eaning

Caritas — Latin for Love

Pomus — Latin for Fruit Tree

Dare — Italian for Give

Conscenzo — Italian for Knowledge

Alba — Italian for dawn, break of day

Coniglio — Italian for Rabbit

Agninas — Latin for Lamb

Dolce — Italian for Gentle

Speranza — Italian for Hope

Spes — Latin for Hope

Optare — Latin for Choose or Choice

Anthony — Priceless Gift (from book of names)

About the Author

Dawn Billings, M.A. believes that her most defining role is that of a mother. She has two great sons, to which her books, and her life are dedicated. Tony is 24, and Corbin is 15. Dawn is founder, and President, of To Touch A Life, Inc., a company dedicated to touching lives in ways that change the direction of hearts and create a better world. Dawn is a highly sought after speaker and trainer who specializes in entitlement issues that are currently plaguing our society. Dawn has been in private practice for fifteen years as a licensed professional counselor, working with individuals, couples, and what she loves most, families.

Dawn's oldest son Tony graduated from USC with a computer engineering degree and is preparing for law school. Dawn's youngest son Corbin is in high school. By the time Corbin was 11-years-old he had won the JC Penny Volunteer of the Year award for getting 169,105 trees planted in Oklahoma, and was chosen by McDonalds, Disney and UNESCO as a Millennium Dreamer in 2000. He has written four books, and continues to be a straight A student, a youth and environmental advocate, and is the youngest professional member in the history of the National Speakers Association.

For more information about Dawn speaking for your church, business, or organization, please contact:

To Touch A Life, Inc.
918-299-3296
www.RelationshipAdviceThatWorks.com
www.ToTouchALife.com
E-mail: ToTouchALife@aol.com